CARRIERS OF

EUNOIA

By: Daze Evander

CARRIERS OF EUNOIA

The characters and events portrayed in this book are fictitious. Any similarity to real persons, living or dead, is coincidental and not intended by the author.

First Edition: December 2020

ISBN-13: 979-8-9854845-0-2 (Paperback)

ISBN-13: 979-8-9854845-2-6 (Hardback)

ISBN-13: 979-8-9854845-3-3 (eBook)

Library of Congress Control Number: 2021925855

Published by Faction Realm Press

www.factionrealmpress.com

To everyone who supported me:

you know who you are - I love you.

CONTENTS

LIST OF ACKNOWLEDGEMENTS:

Front and Back Cover: **James Child**

Character Portraits: **Kevin Sardinha**

Planet Map: **Kkalmighty**

Thank you three for your amazing artwork.

PLANET MAP

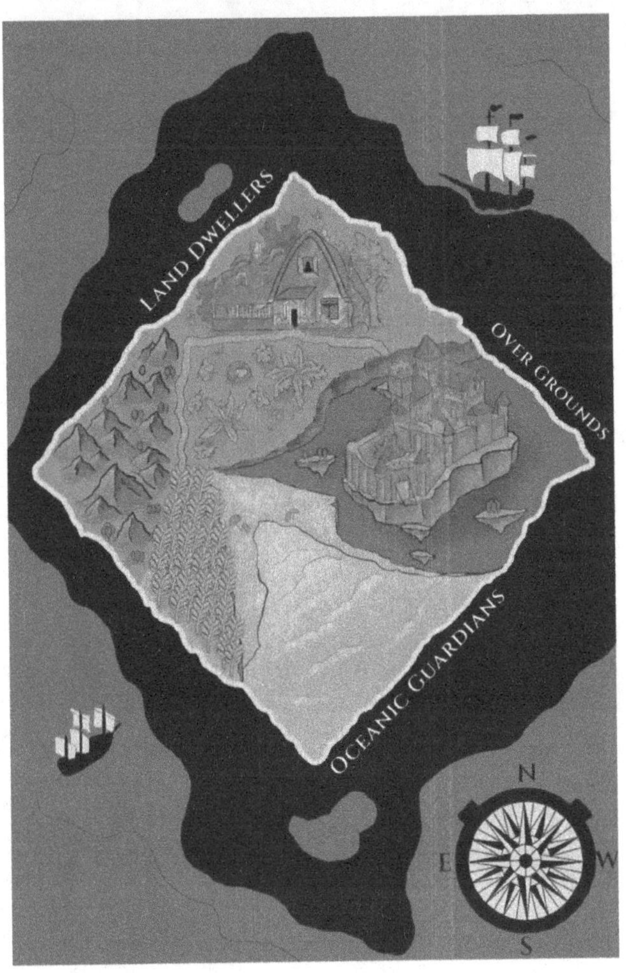

CHAPTER ONE: GUILTY BY ASSOCIATION

Amira

Present

"You all need to step back! Can't you see that this is a crime scene?" My partner, Arcadia, shook her head in disbelief at the crowd of curious individuals who had been overstepping their boundaries. "Get away from the area!"

"People have a very difficult time minding their own business." I said in a hushed tone, tightening my gloves as I watched her give them a quelling look.

Mossy rocks surrounded the two of us as we apprehensively stood near one another. It was a frigid evening and the atmosphere made me tense up with tightened muscles and a clenched jaw. Despite all of my previous traveling, I hadn't yet been to a small town with the type of scenic views that this one had. When I received the call about the case we were investigating, I was surprised that it was located at a layered waterfall near a neighborhood park and next to buildings that others lived in. I glanced at a couple of the windows for a brief moment and noticed some people staring back at me. A small chill scurried up my spine as I pushed my teeth against one another harder.

"Is something wrong?" Arcadia asked me.

"No, just some faces watching us from up there." I pointed to the glass where I was being observed but she didn't look over to see.

"Don't worry about it. There will always be onlookers that refuse to get on with the rest of their day out of morbid curiosity when something like this happens."

My eyes locked with someone else's in the shadow of a room. They were on the third story and wouldn't break their eye contact as I stared. I felt on edge as I saw a grin spreading across their face.

"Where is the body?" I asked Arcadia.

"Right over here." she responded and the stranger who was looking at me shifted their gaze to the deceased victim behind us. They grinned again.

"Someone is smiling in our direction." I tried to warn my partner.

"Don't be so paranoid, people act weird here, they sort of have a reputation of odd behavior."

I forced myself to look away and pay closer attention to the crime scene instead. I followed behind Arcadia as the sound of rushing water dominated my senses. *Something is wrong...* I couldn't help but think to myself and the words started to repeat in my mind. I fumbled with the zipper on my outfit momentarily.

"Make sure you get clear photos. You look like you're shaking right now." Arcadia started to look around. "Where is your camera?"

"It's in my bag, I'll grab it." I tried to snap out of my worried state. I walked towards the gear we had with us and got a hold of what I needed to take the pictures.

Something is wrong... I felt like I was being followed. I turned around and looked behind me, but no one was there.

"Alright Amira, the victim is right here. Let's get some shots; I'll document the clues we have." Arcadia started to scribble notes down as I approached the body.

"Two sets of footprints..." I heard her mutter to herself as I crouched down next to her.

I felt compelled to look up at the window again to see if the stranger was still staring at me but when I did, they were gone. Although their presence was frightful, it seemed far worse to me that they were not visible in my line of sight anymore. *Something is wrong...*

With a quick snap of a branch, Arcadia and I stood up quickly and attentively. "Who's there?" she called out but was answered only with silence.

I kept my mouth closed as I felt the hair on my arms stand up. A gust of wind whistled past me.

"No one should even be near this area at all." She went back to taking notes. "With the number of issues this town has had here you would think they'd shut it down from the public completely."

Wind started to pick up to speeds around twenty miles per hour as the day was rushing to a close. "What do you think happened based on what we know? What other issues have there been?" I asked her, finding it hard to evaluate the scene on my own. *Think clearer, get yourself together, and make a good impression...*

She turned to look at me and paused. "I forgot that you just moved here. I'll fill you in a bit more. Well, we've had around ten incidents that have occurred near this waterfall in the last two years. Murders and people going missing seem to recur for some reason. It's as if there's something in the water that poisons travelers when they get too close. In this case? A nasty fight broke out and now the mess has to be cleaned up."

My eyes drifted over to the dead body that was a few feet away from us. "A 'fight'?"

"Yes. All clues point towards conflict between this man and another one who managed to escape before the police arrived. Other visitors reported the two yelling and the situation turned physical very quickly."

"That's awful." I didn't know what to say.

"It definitely is Amira." The waterfall roared loudly as Arcadia knelt down by the deceased man with her notepad in hand. "Strangulation."

There was a foul smell in the air as the victim's body was lying in a pool of stagnant water. I looked into the camera's viewfinder and zoomed in. Thick bugs were crawling over the man's face and into his mouth, I also noticed the tail end of something that was starting to push its way into his ear canal. I frowned as I took a snapshot with my right pointer finger. These were not the types of photos I dreamed of taking when I was growing up, but I accepted the career I had. *Help solve mysteries. Make mom and dad proud.*

"You said that people have gone missing here in the past... have any of them been found?" I asked, forcing my voice to come out in a steady manner.

"What do you think?" Arcadia's red bangs that framed her face stood out amongst the green shades of the moss behind her. "They were never spotted after visiting this location."

I decided to not continue asking questions and went back to taking more photos. I couldn't shake the feeling that I was being stalked. Every small sound was setting off my intuition, *something is wrong...* The wind was making it difficult to hear everything else that was going on near us. I looked back on one of the photos I had taken of the victim and felt like my insides turned upside down when the man's eyes seemed to have been focused on the camera lens. *That wouldn't make sense...* I had taken the photo from the side and he was on his back with empty eyes pointed up at the sky. I needed to take a second to calm down. *You're overthinking this. Stay strong. Do this job and do it well. Stay collected.*

I stepped away from the caution tape and closer to the waterfall itself. It was only my second week on the job, and I was trying to hold my emotions inside myself until I got home. There was something about this case that seemed different than the others I had already worked on. My attention shifted towards the large trees that loomed over us and the power of the water as it rushed along fiercely. I was careful to not slip on the damp soil as I walked near the side of the waterfall, stepping over wet and unsteady rocks to get a better view.

"Hey! Be careful over there!" I heard Arcadia shout out.

"I will be." I responded, though I don't think I spoke loud enough for her to hear me. There was a bright light that I saw shimmering near the waterfall. "I think I found something so I'm going to check it out."

She didn't respond as I continued towards the light that I assumed was golden rays of the sun colliding against droplets. I steadied myself against a wall of rocks next to me, but found nothing out of the ordinary to see. I felt my eyebrows furrow as I tried to find the source of the sparkle. I walked around the side of the waterfall and let out a deep sigh as I shook my head and turned around to look at the falling water that was now behind me. I knew that I needed to get my mind in the right place to work efficiently, to not be distracted or caught off guard by others. It was hard to not daydream. I found myself wanting to think back on memories I had in my previous line of work. Starting to shiver from the cold water nearby I decided to step towards the pathway next to the crime scene.

The trees that made a large circle around the area were being pulled around by the wind, which was beautiful, but paired with the melancholy atmosphere and tragic event that took place, they made me feel uneasy. As I looked at the rows of trees before me, I noticed a sparkle appear again. I stepped towards it and my entire body went cold as I was met with an unfamiliar and haunting face staring back at me from the darkened area of the forest. A man with bizarre shaky eyes smiled and stood still.

"W-who are you?" I stuttered.

He lunged forwards in a way that could not have been fully human and grabbed me by my neck tightly. I was startled by the amount of distance between us that he was somehow able to physically close with one jump. As I got a closer look at his face, I noticed that his eyes seemed as if they were buzzing with anticipation as he put his hand up to my neck. I tried to yell out for help, but couldn't due to what seemed like an electrical current choking me. I was yanked backwards and I could feel small rocks and branches scraping against my back, legs, and arms as I was tugged along. My skin was being scratched open and I couldn't get a proper breath of air.

"Good luck getting back here." he grumbled quietly.

All went dark around me as I passed out. When I finally awoke, I could still feel a stinging sensation around the base of my neck. I coughed as I started to look around at where the man had taken me. As more moments passed, I realized I was lying down on grass and lifted my head to survey my surroundings. I tried to look for anyone else close by and it initially appeared that I was alone. When I pushed myself up from the ground, I felt a sharp thumping in my head which caused my vision to blur. I could only see endless amounts of hills over hills nearby and when I looked behind me, I saw even more of them.

I reached to grab my phone and only found an empty pocket and my camera was gone. A rush of panic flew over my body as I desperately cried out for help. Echoes of my own scared voice was all I heard in return and I began running. I ran down the first hill that I was on. My legs were moving so quickly that I almost fell several times. I kept going as I approached the next climb and went up the hill despite not having much energy left. I continued to push my efforts to get to the top. I was unable to find anything once I finally got there since it was exactly like the one I had woken up on. The next hill was even higher and I decided to force myself to get on top of it in hopes that I might be able to get a better view of my surroundings. I was sore, out of breath, and only halfway through making my way up the face of it when I almost let go. I doubted myself and my ability to make it. I let out a deep breath and told myself to keep pushing. Even if I accomplished nothing, I could still try.

Six Years Before

"I swear you're one of the best additions to our team, Amira." the head photographer boasted. "You have an eye for the world that no one else does. How long have you been doing photography?"

"When I got my first camera from my parents at age six. I've loved taking photos ever since then."

"Wow and you're nineteen years old now? You've been doing photography for thirteen years? That's incredible. Your practice really shows itself in your work."

"Thank you." Amira noticed the colors changing in the sky as the day was coming to a close. "We're about to hit the golden hour. We can get some great landscape shots just over that river."

The team of seven photographers grabbed the gear to set their cameras up ahead of them.

"I also always wanted to travel when I was younger, especially in high school. Now that I'm in college this really is the perfect opportunity for me to pursue my dream."

"We are glad we awarded you this internship. You truly had one of the most creative perspectives on environmental shifts and seasons out of all of the candidates who applied. You have an eye for observation, that's for sure."

"Thank you. I try my best to appreciate my surroundings. Tampering in journalism sounds fun too." Amira placed her tripod on the ground and adjusted her camera's settings.

"You write? I don't remember you mentioning that in your application."

"It's sort of a new development. I feel a bit more introverted compared to extroverted and I normally don't share much through words. Although I like telling stories with photography, I feel as though I'd like to open up one day with words and maybe use them to portray the depth of the world that I see. Nature tells us a lot about itself silently, we just have to take the time to appreciate it and then we will learn the message it's trying to convey."

Present

I had talked myself into getting to the top of the hill. I didn't think I would reach it, but I had no other choice than to keep going. After I regained my composure, I looked out in all directions. Far off in the distance I could see water past the other mounds of grass and a brighter green area with what looked to be a broken structure in the middle of it. I needed to move quickly in hopes of finding anyone else before it grew too dark to see. By the time I got to the end of the grassy area I had woken up in, a storm had been born and the sky was filled with asperitas clouds, making it look as though ocean waves were above me. Where I was didn't make any sense; it seemed as though I was the only human being there... but some part of my mind knew that wasn't the case.

I made my way down the edge of the last hill I had encountered and spotted a small group of people in the distance near an ocean. I started yelling their way hoping that they would notice and help me figure out what was going on. They said something back in reply, but I couldn't understand their words from where I was. With what little energy I had left I jogged lightly towards the distorted outlines of people that I could see. I was able to make out five silhouettes and I continued to approach them even though they may have been a threat. I had nowhere to go. I knew that the risk was worth taking so I went ahead and began walking over to them. Soon I noticed that they were also coming over to meet me halfway.

"Who are you?" I heard one of them yell out clearly. Thanks to closing some of our distance I understood him.

"I'm not here to hurt you! I'm lost and looking for safety." I put both my hands in the air just in case. "Can any of you help me?"

When I saw their faces, I realized that I was right–five of them were in front of me. From what I could see, the group who I was approaching looked to be around my age. One of the members stood out from the rest as he walked in front of them and led the way towards me. His jet-black hair was almost invisible in the night and swept over his forehead, only slightly covering his curious eyes.

"I'm Anon. It's honestly very nice to meet someone else. I heard you're also looking for help?" He turned to those he was with. "I have with me Saige, Zekiel, Omar, and Zayika who I met earlier. We all ran into one another and have been traveling as a group, wandering aimlessly for what has felt like forever. What's your name?"

"I'm Amira, it's nice to meet you too." I reached forward to shake his hand as I looked at the four behind him. "I'm glad to meet you all as well."

"Do you have any idea where we are or what is going on?" he asked me.

"Unfortunately, I don't. I was going to ask if any of you did."

The five seemed timid as they looked around.

"We're just as clueless as you seem to be, sorry. We've been trying to get our hands on some weapons along with shelter, food, and water."

They all looked fatigued with dry skin and cracked lips. "How long have you been walking exactly?"

"We've lost track of the hours now. We woke up on these hills and have been without a clue ever since. I'm not sure where we are, I don't even think we're on Earth."

"You don't know that for sure." the man named Omar stated.

"My intuition is telling me otherwise." Anon bit his lip as his eyes searched over my body. "You don't have any weapons, do you?"

"No I don't. Why?" *Are we in danger?*

Anon pointed off in the distance towards what looked to be a jungle. "We've heard some fighting, people yelling at one another, specifically in that direction. I feel like we need to be able to protect ourselves in case anything bad happens." He looked at me almost longingly as he spoke. "Do you want to join us?"

"Sure, it's better to travel as a growing group than to do it alone, right?"

"Exactly. We need to find some cover. I've been telling everyone that I thought I saw a lighthouse a bit farther out. I'm going to swim over to it and see what I can find."

The woman standing next to him looked aggravated. She had wavy hair that was white on the top and then faded down to purple by her shoulders. She tapped on his arm and shook her head at him. "You shouldn't do that, Anon. Do you actually know how unsafe that is?"

I didn't disagree with her. The storm had already seemed to have gotten worse in the short amount of time it took us all to meet and the height and speed of the waves intensified greatly. The wind grew faster too and stung our faces painfully as it swept past us.

"Staying out here in the open and not finding anything we need is just as unsafe, Zayika. I need to do this." he replied as he faced the ocean off to his right. "It's not like we have many options, and we need to find someone who can offer us any help that we can get. Right now this is our best chance. Unless any of you have a better idea?"

We all stood silently.

"That's what I assumed." Anon made his way over to the water with all of us reluctantly following and braced himself for cold contact.

He gave us one last look before making his way into it gradually until he eventually was submerged up to his shoulders. He started swimming as well as he could and dove into the raging waves that were plummeting towards him.

"Wait," Omar said, "didn't he say something earlier about not being the best swimmer? I swear there's always someone that has to try to show off."

With huge intakes of air, Anon tried his best to keep a steady pace and remain in the direction of what he believed was a lighthouse. We watched on nervously. *Is the lighthouse even real?* All we could see from where we stood was a bright shining light in the ocean. Anon looked as though he became lightheaded with his body struggling against the current. His swimming efforts substantially decreased in speed. I imagined salt water was stinging his eyes as he searched for how much farther he needed to go. Time felt like it was dragging on as the five of us waited to see what would happen. I was surprised to see someone make such an intense decision with very little hesitation. *Is he trying to prove something to the group he had been with?*

There seemed to be something about Anon that told me he wanted to be brave and seem fearless to everyone else. I could sense his fear though, it was very evident due to the way he was carrying himself. I had only just met him but felt like I had already known him for a while. *He wants to try to lead this group he's with, doesn't he?* I looked over at the other four who were seeing him venture into the rising waves.

Zayika didn't seem to be on edge with him risking his life the way that he was as she let out many exasperated sighs. "He really thinks he's doing something amazing, doesn't he?" She looked down at her fingernails to check the polish on them.

"Anon always thinks he's doing something amazing." Omar shrugged. "This is his, what, fifth act of bravery by now?"

Exactly how long have this group of five been traveling together before I arrived?

Eventually Anon was right in front of the glowing light, it seemed so bright I assumed he could barely see. He started yelling incoherently. I wasn't sure what to do but watch on and take note of the others' reactions. Zekiel was looking directly ahead, not making any movements, and had broad shoulders that were right below his blonde hair. He was standing very close to the last member of the group who was named Saige. She acted utterly enthralled by Zekiel as she held onto his arm tightly. She was shorter than him and was looking up at his face more than at Anon, who was out in the menacing ocean.

As I turned my attention back on Anon, I noticed that his only choice was to get back to shore. I think he then dove under the water to try and desperately hold his breath long enough to get away from what he found. He yanked himself up towards the surface and yelled out in terror that he saw a giant bulging eye belonging to an unknown creature watching him. Anon was gasping for air as he made his best attempt to swim back to everyone else on shore, but the jolting water hindered him. He tried his best to not look back as he yelled at the top of his lungs for us to help.

"Hold on!" Zayika shrieked back at him with irritation and then looked at me and the rest. "I'm going after him. I knew this was a bad idea!"

I watched as she ran and dove into the water. *She's quick on her feet.* Zayika thankfully was a fast swimmer and made her way over to him as quickly as she could.

"We're going to be okay, right Zeek?" I heard Saige ask Zekiel as she was batting her eyelashes at him.

"I don't know." he replied plainly with reserved and tense body language.

I then witnessed something large rising up above Anon as he swam frantically. There was a creature that I had never seen before. I was only able to see a part of its body for a short amount of time until it disappeared under the ocean again in an attempt to get a hold of Anon. I heard him cry out in fear as he disappeared beneath the waves before all of our eyes. Going after him, Zayika got near where he was, and she too instantly vanished. The unfortunate sounds of screaming from the water rang out and we all assumed the worst. I told myself that this was just another twisted dream I was having. *I'm only in a dream.* Sadly, I was wrong. I closed my eyes for a few moments and tried to wake up from where I was.

"Keep moving!" Zayika shouted as she held him with her left arm and fought against the waves with her right.

"I can't see where I'm going!" Anon responded.

"I don't care, I've got you. Just don't stop trying to swim!"

The pair were somehow outswimming something gigantic that was lurking within the ocean's deep trenches. *There's no way they are faster than whatever is down there. Something else must be going on down below...*

"It seems like everyone is saving each other's lives besides Anon." Omar stated. "He hasn't saved anyone since we all got here."

"Maybe that's why he's trying so hard to do that now." I responded. For some reason Omar seemed surprised that I replied to him as he lifted his bushy eyebrows and decided to become quiet around me after that small exchange.

When they were closer to the shore, we all waded out to grab a hold of them. I saw Anon droop almost lifelessly by Zayika's side.

"Speak to us. Are you okay?" I took his pale face in my hands and watched him about to fade out of consciousness. "Don't pass out."

The rest of the group crowded around as I held onto him. I wrapped my arms around his upper half and kept his head elevated. I felt comfortable embracing Anon, like I was checking up on a familiar friend and I felt a need to look out for him. "Are you hurt anywhere? I don't see blood."

"I think it was the lip of the creature that got a hold of me! It was slippery, cold, and felt like bumpy rubber trying to grip onto my leg. I didn't feel any teeth thankfully." Anon managed to spurt out. "I'm alright. Just not the best swimmer."

"Clearly." Omar stated while hovering over him.

"No one asked for your input, Omar." he managed to say back.

"Well no one asked you to try to take on the role of being the hero here."

I lightly motioned Omar aside to break them up. "We have to continue onwards. The worst decision we could make would be to stop moving."

"Did you hear that Anon?" Zayika jumped into the conversation. She was pulling her long, wet hair up and away from her face as she motioned towards him coughing on the ground next to me. "It's possible to make a bad decision. This might be a good teaching moment for you. Frantically throwing yourself out into the ocean to become a fish's next meal was pretty stupid. I don't know who you're trying to impress, because I know it's not me, but knock it off before you get us all killed. You're lucky I saved your life at all."

Anon's expression was kind as he responded to her, "Thanks for that Zayika. I'll never be able to thank you enough." he said with a tender heart.

The rest of us watched and waited for her response. She acted angry, like she was expecting him to try to fight back at her. "Get over yourself, Anon."

The conversation ended after that and the group took my advice, resulting in us walking for many hours from the next early morning to what we believed was the middle of a new day. The saturation of colors around us was almost overwhelming to see. The place we were at was gorgeous to look at and terrifying to walk along at the same time. I spotted the hills we were on, what looked to be a large field, and then the terrain breaking off into three major sections. Besides our group of six, there wasn't another person in sight. I found moments where I was longing to check what time it was only to be reminded that it seemed to be irrelevant. I was starving and lightheaded. The sun was beaming down on us heavily as we searched for somewhere safer than out in the open to rest, which became a seemingly impossible goal as more time passed.

"Let's give up." I heard Omar say next to me. We left the hills and slowly made our way into one of the three main areas filled with many trees, leaves, and vines. I didn't want to stop making progress and felt as though we needed more cover to rest safely. "Can we stay and catch our breath here please?" he asked desperately.

Zekiel, who was walking behind Omar, completely spoke up for the first time since I met the group, "He's right. We don't want to die hoping to escape instead of escaping if we hadn't pushed ourselves too far."

I, along with the rest, reluctantly agreed with him and chose to sit down as we tried to become accustomed to our new surroundings. I rested on warm dirt that was under shade provided by a cluster of fuzzy olive-green branches up above me. Everyone was quiet for a while. It was actually peaceful and beautiful outside. The sunlight shone through the bushes and trees that created unique and lovely patterns engulfing us with calming orange tones. I let out a deep breath and allowed myself to take in the moment I was living in. This was something I'd neglected to do for a while and knew I needed to slow down and put my mind at ease at the fact that we all were alive and safe... *for the time being.*

As I stared up into the sky, I heard someone fall down onto the ground beside me. Surprisingly it was Zekiel and he spoke to me in a hushed manner, apparent to me that he didn't want anyone else to hear what he needed to share.

"Amira, I can't help but feel like something bad is going to happen. We need to change our course of action. You can't look at me seriously and try to tell me that not one part of you doesn't sense that we are in danger right out in the open staying still."

I took in what he said and thought carefully about what to say next. "Why are you telling me this? What am I supposed to do about it? It's not like I'm able to protect us if something happens anyways, but Anon seems like a leader." I stated.

Zekiel ran his calloused hands through his lengthy dirty blonde hair and rested his face on them. He watched everyone else with a look of nothing but deep concern on his face. "I'm telling you this because I think you can. You might be the best shot at leading this group. Anon tries to lead, but I'm not sure he cares enough or is even cut out for that job. I can tell that you have leadership skills by the way you carry yourself and I think he might be lacking that. I honestly don't have the willpower to lead this group. I'm emotionally drained. Looking after myself is hard enough and my only true goal is to protect Saige. We need a plan to get out of here."

"I think Anon shows promise so let's give him time. He has already exemplified bravery and tenacity for taking that risk out in the ocean." I spoke attentively to him. "In regard to creating an escape plan, what could we possibly do to get out of a place without any indication that there's a way to leave? We have no maps and absolutely no clue of where we're headed. The way I was brought here is not a story I want to get into so hopefully we don't have to leave the same way we came." I lightly touched a bruise that had formed on my neck.

"Don't worry. We don't need to share personal details with each other. We don't even have to be close friends. I just came to tell you that a plan needs to be developed. Now I'm not sure, but what if there's some type of passageway or tunnel that can lead us to something useful? Maybe we can craft a device that could guide us home? I don't know. Walking in circles will get us nowhere. We need supplies." Stress radiated from his presence as Zekiel started to walk away from me. "What I do know is that someone is going to have to lead."

Everyone had a look of silent despair on their face as I studied each one of them.

"Let's keep moving forwards." I felt like my words were failing as I stood up. Speaking to a group was uncomfortable for me. "We can't stay here forever and we might be able to pull through this as a team if we work with one another. Even though we don't know where we are going, we could try to find a way out of here. Zekiel agrees with me. He thinks that maybe there could be passageways or tunnels that could be useful. Maybe we'll discover a way to return home."

I heard Zayika laugh off to my right. She kicked the dirt under her feet as she walked over to where I stood proudly. "Did you say 'passageways and tunnels'? Now what do you think is on the other side? How about hidden traps? What about pathways to creatures that are ready to devour us whole?" I got up close to her face and lowered my voice.

"Zayika stop. We need to think positively. Getting everyone scared isn't something we can do." She backed away from me with a smug look and raised her voice.

"So for those of you interested in what she was whispering about, she told me that she doesn't want you all scared. Pretty ridiculous right? Why tell the truth when we can just lie to ourselves? We all need to just hold hands, believe together, and hope for the best for good things to happen." Her words were coated in sarcasm. "Grow up Amira. Zekiel, you need to learn to speak up; Anon, you need to learn to sit down, and I'll throw Omar into this attack simply because he complains too much. We're obviously screwed. Cut the childish talk out. Let's all at least try to be real here instead of creating new problems with false hope. At least Saige seems to know how to keep her mouth shut. I mean, she's too busy looking at Zekiel to talk to any of the rest of us."

Saige blushed with a horrified look.

"Zayika might be making a small point here... we need to be realistic." Anon interjected.

Zekiel tugged onto Anon's shoulder and spun him around backwards. "So what is your bright idea? Just camp out indefinitely and wait for something to attack you again? At least we're trying to do something productive Anon. Not just sit around all day or jump directly into danger's mouth. At least some of us want to be hopeful and think critically."

I could tell that Anon was taken aback by Zekiel at first, but regained his composure swiftly. "You're right. I said we should be 'realistic,' but don't get my words twisted, I never said that we should lose hope. I swam out in the ocean because I was trying to take action, but we haven't even found food or water yet. Let's step back and start with the basics. We can't be on a mission to kill ourselves. Maybe your passageway idea is true, but we also can't march into anything without being rational and taking our time checking for threats at this point. At least there was a light that I had to concretely guide me. You don't have a sign to support your theory. Are you on a suicide mission?"

As soon as he finished talking, Zekiel landed an unrestrained punch across his face which knocked him backwards.

"Don't ever talk that way to me again. You don't know anything about me. You're the one who just swam out into oblivion to try to prove a point so that's pretty tough talk coming from you. Just because your idea failed doesn't mean that mine will. How dare you stand up to defend Zayika's words?"

I saw a hint of frustration in Anon's eyes. "I wasn't trying to defend her completely, I ju-"

I got in between both of them, worried that Anon would try to strike back against Zekiel, but he walked away while tending to his bruising face. Everyone stared at Zekiel as if they wanted to say something but couldn't figure out what it was.

Saige made her way over to us and placed her hand on Zekiel's back. "Ignore Anon, alright? He doesn't know what he's talking about and never seems to, if anyone is weak it's him. I think you're the one who's right. We should keep going." They both walked off together and I was unable to hear what they said after that.

I had started to become more concerned than I already had been about escaping. The small group I was in already seemed to have started falling apart and picking sides against one another which was one of the worst things we could do if we wanted any hope of surviving.

"Well I'm moving onwards. Anyone who wants to follow has the option to." I spoke unconfidently.

Omar, Zayika, Zekiel and Saige decided to travel behind me. We left the comfortable and shaded area to continue off into the more tangled part of the jungle. Anon watched nearby as we all took off and after thinking for a moment he decided to follow, still keeping some distance between himself and us. He was quiet for a little while which seemed challenging for him. Not too long after that he started talking again, "Just for the record, I think tha–"

Zekiel turned around to face him with a look full of distaste. "Anon, contrary to what you seem to believe, none of us care what you think."

I tugged on his shirt quickly to try to get him to stop talking. "Do you really need to make anything worse with him? We're unsafe enough without turning on each other. Creating drama is the last thing we need, Zekiel."

They both refused to say anything else after that and we all had progressively gotten more tired and famished as time passed by.

"We need to find food soon, guys. Does anyone know how long we've been walking?" Omar said.

"None of us have any idea. I don't think that matters here." Zayika replied as she looked up at the stars that came into view. "Guess now we know that it's nighttime."

"Hopefully we will survive until dawn..." Anon stated. "Anyone? Come on, please tell me at least one of you got that reference."

"Well I'm going to hang back for a little while or else I think I'll collapse. You all can continue on without me, I'll catch up later." Omar placed his left hand out to lean onto a wide tree next to him when he tripped slightly and slid downwards. He gave out a small cry of pain and we all went back to check on him.

"You're bleeding." I told him as I watched blood falling down his hand. "What happened?"

"I don't know. There's something sharp right here. Can someone help me bandage this please? I hope it doesn't get infected." he said while wincing on the ground and being stepped over by Anon. "Hey! Don't put your feet near me!"

"I'm trying to find out what cut you." Anon said as he slowly touched at the vines that covered the base of the tree. He took a large handful of them that were near Omar's blood and pulled them off. His expression lightened up. "I found something! Everyone look."

I walked next to him and my eyes followed to where he was pointing. Beneath the leaves there was what looked to be a doorknob. It was rusted all over, probably unusable, but it looked like a small sign of hope for us. I called Zekiel over to see it and I could tell he thought the same as me. *Progress.*

"I'll tear off more vines. Let's hope it will open." Anon got excited as he began clearing more vegetation out of the way.

"How safe is this?" Omar said in almost a whisper as I began turning the handle on the worn-out metal door in front of us.

I stopped for a moment to see the looks of everyone behind me then pushed the knob forwards so that we could discover what was inside. I had to force the door open with a strong push. The metal creaked loudly in the middle of all the silence surrounding us. I tried to prepare myself for any surprises. "I think it's safe." I spoke with slight disbelief. *Get it together. Trust your own words...*

Through the door there was a passageway that led underground. As I placed my right foot on the first step of the set of stairs, I felt a hand on my shoulder as I heard Anon's voice. "I'll go first." I chose to not question him. I assumed he'd want to redeem himself in the eyes of everyone else after what had happened with Zekiel earlier in the day, so I let him go ahead of me. I could tell he was more nervous than I was. Shakily, he went forwards to uncover what was hiding below. It appeared that we had found an underground bunker. The light from outside was enough to brighten a pathway for him to be guided down into.

Anon continued down the small set of stairs that led to an empty hallway. "Don't follow me yet. You all should wait until I see what's around the corner."

The suspense was killing me. I didn't want this to become the lighthouse situation all over again. Moments that felt like hours passed by. We realized that nothing was lurking in the darkness when we saw Anon give us a wave of safety guiding us to come in after him.

"I hope none of you are claustrophobic." Immediately we discovered what he meant by that. The passageway through the chilly bunker was extremely narrow. With each step it felt as though the walls were closing in tighter against our sides. With a right turn we entered a room filled with boxes and shelves loaded with medical supplies and food. There was even part of a bed that could be seen in the far corner of the next room from where we had come from.

"You all are welcome, by the way." Anon said proudly.

"I'm the one who found this. Get over yourself, man." Omar replied tiredly as he searched in a metal container for something that could sterilize his wound. "I need to find some medical supplies."

Zayika scoffed, "That was barely a scratch, you will be fine." She pointed to the next room. "I wonder what's in there?"

"I don't know, why don't you go find out? Hopefully we'll come across some weapons. I'm not seeing any right here so far." Anon shoved anything he found into his jacket and also began filling his arms with as much as he could carry. "Make sure you let me know what you find before you take anything. It's only fair, seeing as though I was the first to scope everything out for safety." I could tell he was making an attempt to joke with everyone.

Silent minutes went by of us looting the bunker until Anon jumped in again to create conversation. "Are any of you completely sure we aren't dreaming right now?" he asked.

"If we were, we would've already woken up." I said directly.

"I don't know about that, some dreams of mine have lasted for a really long time."

I barely heard what he had said to me as I looked through a small stack of crates. "Yeah, okay, that's cool." I couldn't help but still be entirely overwhelmed by the unsteady state of everything happening around us. "I'm not seeing any weapons."

"Wanna hear about one specific crazy dream I had that I will never forget?"

"Maybe we could use this bunker for shelter, it's cold here but I don't mind. We'll need to check all the rooms. I think this is a good option for now." Zayika disregarded Anon on purpose as she clung to the milky white fabric of the woven cardigan over her tank top.

"No one cares about my dream?" Anon sighed. "It's a great story."

"Tell us later on. I'm sure we'll have a lot of time together." I replied.

Omar was breathing into his palms and rubbing his hands frantically together. "Not if we die soon."

"Let me change the subject and tell you guys about it. Alright, so I dreamt that I was in the middle of the ocean. The water looked like ink and rain was pouring down on me. I wasn't swimming–"

"That's good." Omar cut him off and laughed. "We all know that's not your greatest gift."

"Yeah, because me almost dying is so funny. What if that had been you? What if–"

I chimed in. "Continue your story Anon."

"Fine. Okay so I wasn't in the water, but I was on this jagged rock that was just large enough for me to rest on. I was sitting down with my arms wrapped around my legs and my face rested on my knees. I heard a loud roar in the air and felt a sting course through my body. I watched my arms start lighting up a neon blue color. I put them out in front of me and saw lighting actually flowing through myself."

Omar was the only one who was laughing again. "Are you on drugs, man?"

"I'm being completely serious. That's when my dream ended. Strangely enough, and the craziest thing was, I actually felt something burning within me when I woke up."

"I ask this again... are you on drugs?" Omar said with crossed arms.

"You 'felt something'?" Saige seemed the most interested. "When did you have this dream?"

"When I first arrived here. That's what I woke up to actually."

Up until then I hadn't seen her give anyone else but Zekiel her undivided attention. "I had one similar to it."

Anon shrugged his shoulders and turned to get back to looting. "Whatever, if you all want to mock me that's fine. I remember what I saw and felt."

"Hey, hold on, I'm not making fun of you if that's what you think." She walked around a metal table to get closer to him. "I really did have one of my own. I was standing in a room and every surface around me was various shades of green. There was no noise and I stood there quietly for a long time. Before I knew it there was an earthquake that had started. The ground beneath me shook relentlessly. I fell over and when I landed, I felt a sharp jolt of pain in my face and then I was awake."

He looked down at her and noticed the hint of honest intensity in her eyes. "You're telling the truth?"

"Of course. There's no point in lying about something like that."

Omar seemed bothered and asked, "Why didn't either of you bring this up until just now?"

Anon shoved his hands into his pockets and neither of the two replied for a few seconds. "I guess I didn't because it's sort of unsettling. Everyone is on edge enough already just being here, I didn't want to make anyone even more worried or think that there was something wrong with me." He looked over at Saige to get her response. "You?"

"I don't know, back at home I would always have weird dreams. I just didn't read into any of it too much." She watched Zekiel as she spoke for some reason.

I didn't give a response to what everyone was saying. I was more invested in the remaining rooms of the bunker that hadn't been checked yet. After hearing some of the yelling that Anon had referred to earlier, I knew we needed weapons desperately. A shocking discovery startled me as I finally examined the bed seen out from one of the doorways.

"We need to leave right now." I told the group. "Someone else is here. There's a man sleeping on the mattress."

"Sleeping? Then we have some time. He must be a heavy sleeper if he hasn't heard us by now. Oh come on Zekiel, you can't carry more than that?" Zayika said with a mouth full of packaged food she had already started eating.

"No you don't understand. He has a gun." Worriedly I leaned forward and pulled the door to the room closed. I winced when the metal had collided too loudly. We heard the man ask who was there as we began to scatter around the bunker rapidly.

We quickly took as much of his food and supplies as we could before we ran back outside. As I climbed onto the first step, I could hear him yell from the inside, "You're lucky this time that I'm hurt, but soon enough I'll be right behind you. Watch your back!" I kept looking straight ahead as I ran up the stairs with supplies almost spilling out of my clothes. We ran under the night sky for a long time until we felt like we could safely walk again.

The number of trees around us eventually faded away as we pressed onward, moving closer back to the ocean.

CHAPTER TWO: BIOLUMINESCENCE

Amira

Present

After advancing over a stretch of land on foot during the night, we approached a gigantic field of wheat that spread onwards and side to side so far that we couldn't see the end of it. It was abnormally large and towered over us, it could have been used as a perfect hiding place if we had needed it to be. We ventured inside and wandered through it until it became morning, trying to push stems away from our faces as we went. Time was passing fast. There were moments when we felt like we were in a hay maze, resulting in us losing track of which way we had already gone. We went in circles several times. The day was fleeting as evening approached. As I looked through the wheat stems in front of me, I noticed that we had reached the final section of the field and saw we were close to the ocean. This encouraged us to keep moving forward.

We all came to a standstill at a cliff which abruptly ended our journey. I steadied my feet into the rocks below me so I could look over the edge without falling. I noticed a section off to the side with an open area of sand that we could rest in to catch our breaths. "I found somewhere we can stay for right now. We'll have to get down this cliff first and make our way over there." I motioned for the rest of the group to come see what I was talking about. "See that leveled out ledge? The one before the second smaller cliff near the ocean? We'll probably be safe there."

"Let's settle down here for a little while." Omar said as he began organizing all that we had grabbed from the bunker.

"There's an old canoe!" Zayika noticed. "Looks like it was abandoned over by the water."

All of us attentively made our way down to the ledge and Zayika and I wasted no time in using the canoe we had found. I was looking forward to getting away from the chaos for a little while on the calming, and almost reassuring, rhythm of the waves.

"You two be careful. Remember what happened last time we were by the water?" Anon asked with a concerned glance.

"Don't worry. We aren't going out far." I replied as I stepped onto the wobbly canoe's surface. *Zekiel was wrong about Anon– he does care...* "Just getting away for a little while." The sun had already started to set and filled the clouds with a soft shade of orange slowly mixing with rose gold. No one said anything else for a little while. The times with everyone quiet had turned out to be my favorite. We all seemed to bask in comfortable silence for a change. I rested on the edge of the canoe with my legs extended in front of me in a small pool of water that had fallen into it. While letting out a deep sigh I placed my arm on the wooden ridge next to me and let my hand fall into the ocean.

"Do you think we're going to die?" Zayika asked too calmly as she sat across from me.

"I don't know."

She grabbed a piece of her wavy purple hair and twisted it around her finger. "I think we're going to."

"We picked up enough supplies to live on for at least a while so maybe we'll find more as we go along. There might be more bunkers."

"Even if we did, what about the other things that exist here? You know we aren't alone. With no way to defend ourselves I'll give us another day maybe."

"Thinking that way will get you killed, Zayika."

"No. Lying to yourself the way that you do will."

I uncomfortably glanced away from her and saw the rest of our group relaxing on the sand. They dug into their snacks as they finally felt stable enough to put some effort into getting to know each other more. The only one who seemed to not be making any effort was Omar who didn't fit in very well. The people I met seemed bright and I felt like Zayika was wrong. A part of my mind told myself that somehow we'd make it through whatever challenge we would face. *I'd at least give us more than just a few measly days of survival.*

I tried to think of something to say to not only lighten the mood but also change the conversation. "What life will you be returning to when you get home?"

She looked at me with distaste. "You mean if I get home? I'll be going back to a busy life. I know a lot of people and when I have free time, I'm usually running around all over town with them."

"That's great. Kind of exactly opposite from me, actually."

"What do you enjoy doing?"

That was an easy question. "When I was younger, I did photography as my main hobby, but now I have a career as a crime scene investigator. My dad was a CSI too... I wanted to make him proud."

Zayika gave me a doubtful look. "Let's see you put those skills to use here then."

As we spoke, I began to feel something rumbling the boat as it rose up from below us. I sprang up and looked at my feet as we were jolting side to side.

"What's that?" Zayika asked, holding firmly onto my shoulder to steady herself.

"I have no idea." I scanned over the waters for a few moments until I noticed a dark green color start appearing.

We tried desperately to grab our paddles to start rolling back to shore, but we ran out of time and were too far out. We watched as a large box with moss growing on it started to come to the surface. Zayika and I glanced over at those on land who weren't saying anything.

I leaned slightly over the boat and reached my hand out until Omar shrieked out, "Don't touch it!" I heard him get hit in the chest by Anon.

"What's wrong with you Omar? You're going to make her fall in the wat–" I traced an invisible line running from Anon's enlarging eyes to the unfamiliar sound that was slowly building up behind me.

I stood in shock at what was there. Coming out of the metal box was what looked to be a cross between a woman and a fish-like creature. She hovered above the box, her scaly skin was a light blue and transparent enough to see the veins beneath it. I could see blood traveling within her entire body, her ribs, and even her heart beating. She had long green hair that closely resembled seaweed with harsh eyebrows that framed her fiery eyes. Salty freckles covered her face. *Could she be a mermaid? They exist here?* I glanced down where her legs should be and saw a tail-like appearance to them, long and thin, but it wasn't a complete fin. Her scales got thicker towards the lower half of her body.

"I've finally found you." Her voice was smooth and rippled over us.

"What did it say?" Anon spoke up. "Don't worry, I'll help! Stay still!"

But before he could even take a step forward the creature had thrown her arm out from in front of her. What I could only guess was seaweed spewed out of the palm of her hand like rope and wrapped around his ankle tightly. She yanked him forwards onto the ground and dragged him until he hit the rocks that outlined the shore. "You aren't going anywhere!"

She looked down at me with her glossy unnatural maroon eyes observing me. "But you are." She pointed her right hand at me this time and began speedily wrapping up my entire body in the sticky and leafy material. My body immediately froze up, unable to speak or move, and all I could do was look around frantically before my eyes were covered up too. I could hear that Zayika was yelling as I felt myself being plunged into the depths of the ice-cold ocean.

Six Years Before

"I just don't know if your career goal is realistic." Amira's dad spoke to her through her cell phone. "Maybe you should steer your work path in a different direction and do photography as a backup hobby."

"Photography is important to me. Taking photos of nature is my passion and I don't know how you don't respect it after this many years. You and mom gave me my first camera. You both helped inspire me to look through a different lens and find new angles to view the world with."

"Amira, that was a simple gift that any parents would give their child, years ago we bought that for you. If I had known you were going to run with it the way you have then I would have gotten you something more productive to point you towards a real career."

"You're not understanding where I'm coming from. The leaders of my internship see something valuable in me that I wish you could see too. They think that my photography could really make a difference someday and I might even pursue journalism."

"I just don't agree with your choices. I don't think this internship is a good idea to spend your time or energy on."

"I'm finally getting to see the world and branch out of my shell a little bit. I'm starting to learn how to have and hold conversations with others better."

"I hardly believe that. You barely spoke to me or your mother when you were around."

"Why don't you want to see me grow?"

"I want you to grow in a direction towards something bigger than your own self. Don't limit your capabilities."

"Photography is special, Dad, but if it would make you happy then I can minor in it and focus more on something else. So what is it that you think I'm more fit to do instead?" Amira asked.

"Try to make a difference in someone else's life. I don't know... I just expected more from you." He took a drawn-out pause. "I thought you would take after my career path and make me proud."

"Why didn't you tell me that's what you wanted?"

"I figured you would be inspired by me growing up. As our only child I wanted you to continue on some piece of where you came from. The work that I've done has solved unforeseen mysteries and given many families the answers and closure that they desperately needed. You're here to make a difference, Amira. If I know anything it's that you're here on this Earth for a reason. Make use of your skills for the greater good."

Present

The frigid water turned warmer as I stayed underneath it for a little while. The individual who I believed to have been a mermaid was taking me down with her, deeper and deeper. She removed what was covering my eyes but a bubble of air remained attached to my nose and mouth so I tried to remain calm as I noticed a castle-like structure come into view.

There were all types of plants surrounding it including colorful algae, seaweed, and many types of coral. I even noticed some concrete statues slightly off in the distance behind the building we were going to, but unfortunately couldn't see well enough to figure out what they were made of exactly. A school of small fish scurried past me and the woman laughed at my startled reaction. I was scared as we arrived where she was taking me, and being out in the open amongst any type of sea creature had started to worry me even more.

How is she breathing underwater?

She brought me inside and I was immediately struck in the chest by a man who greeted me through the front door. My lungs burned as it felt as though I was drowning. My skin itched severely as I watched scales grow over it and found myself in the arms of another unknown person and I surprisingly could hear them speaking.

A man spoke to the woman who captured me. "Nice catch Enya. She seems to be taking this morphing process well. She's the one being assigned to the companion, right? I really hope she's not too alarmed by its presence. I wish I was given a pet." He looked at me next. "What is your name?"

"Amira." I told them. There was a total of four of us in the room.

"I'm Orson, that's Enya, and Marcellus is the one holding you up right now so you don't hit the ocean floor. We're your new people. Let's finish your morphing and get you situated." He placed his hands in my direction as a slow hum escaped his fingers. *Everyone has... tails instead of legs?*

The room began spinning hazily as I dozed off into unconsciousness. I can't remember how long I was out. I remember feeling a current pulling me forwards as I started to wake up. The ocean water had felt different to me after being in it for so long. I still struggled with the worry of drowning even though I was apparently given the ability to breathe underwater. Existing the way that I was felt very unnatural. I knew I was farther down into the ocean than anyone should go if they wanted to survive. I didn't feel in control of my own body as I was being guided somewhere away from my apparent new location I was expected to reside in. I tried to start swimming but I felt weak and on the brink of passing out again. *Stay awake.* I noticed that I couldn't feel my toes anymore. When I attempted to kick my feet, I was in shock of the sensation that was created instead–I was given a tail. Orange thick scales had engulfed my legs. I had believed that mermaids were only a myth, and in the most drastic way I had discovered I was wrong.

I started to panic. It was becoming harder for me to breath as the water carried me towards a distant light. The brightness reminded me of what Anon had previously thought was a lighthouse. As its intensity grew, I had to close my eyes as I was scared I would be blinded. I could sense a giant living being near me, but my intuition was telling me to remain calm. With courage I looked towards what was bringing me over to them. The current came to a stop and I had a hard time seeing what it was at first.

The light was now behind me and illuminating what looked to be gigantic teeth within arm's length from where I had been. I tried to count them but failed due to their harrowing size. They were sharp and angled off into different directions. The creature that was before me was the largest I had ever seen in my entire life. I wished I had a camera to document the mystery that was lurking in the shadows. I started to swim backwards in order to get a better view of it and surprisingly, the creature stayed where it was as I did so. As I started to see more, I noticed that its mouth was gaping open and its eyes were fixated on me. I couldn't believe what I saw... it was a massive anglerfish. I felt like my heart had plummeted into my own stomach with this realization and fear of being swallowed alive, torn into pieces, or both. I felt frozen as we both looked at each other with curious eyes. I was scared to swim away. I didn't know what else to do besides speak to it.

"I'm Amira." My voice sounded muffled and unsteady underwater.

The creature let out a low growl and slowly moved towards me.

"You're not going to hurt me, are you?" For some reason I didn't feel nonsensical for speaking to the fish. "Why did you call me here to you?"

The anglerfish started to swim slightly downwards as if it was initiating a bow in front of me. I apprehensively put my hand out to touch its head. Feeling it was unsettling, there was a slimy and uneven texture near its eyes that brushed against my fingertips, but it seemed to remain calm.

"What are you? Some sort of pet?" *Is this fish what the others were referring to?* As I spoke, its eyes shifted upwards at me as it growled again. "Was that supposed to be a 'yes'?"

The fish widened its mouth several times and its fins started to flutter around as if it was excited for me to be speaking to it. By its appearance I could tell that it was in fact a female anglerfish, but some type of overgrown mutation of the species. It started to growl one last time but in a much more menacing tone.

"What's wrong?" I asked, beginning to become fearful of it again.

She swam forwards and lunged to catch a different and smaller unknown creature in its mouth that I didn't even know had been stalking behind me. It must have fallen for the bright light and had become her next meal. Blood filled a part of the water near me as the anglerfish started to eat the other species. I placed both my hands on its head with confidence that surprised me. Alarmingly, the fish and I bonded right away. *I'm safer with this creature by my side.*

"You just protected me. You are my pet, aren't you? I'll name you Hippo. You'll keep looking after me, right?"

Hippo let out an approving loud hum at my words as she ate.

CHAPTER THREE: DYNAMIC DUO

Zekiel

Present

We all stood in absolute horror. I never thought that I would witness the death of someone right in front of me and everything happening had felt unbearable. We had only known Amira for just a short while, but seeing her pulled under the ocean was one of the worst sights that I had seen so far. *There's no way she will make it out alive...* I felt every part of me tense up as I had no choice but to watch waves ripple peacefully despite what had just happened. The only thing that averted my attention was the sound of crying behind me and I immediately knew who it was. I went over and wrapped my arms around her as she started to panic. I barely knew what to say as I had a hard time even calming my own self down. I held Saige close and tried to comfort her the best that I could.

"I'm here for you, okay?" That's all I could manage to say after struggling for a few moments as I fought back tears of my own. I'm sure she knew I was as scared as her by the shakiness in my voice. She grabbed onto me tighter as I felt her nod into my shirt. "I always will be."

Five Years Before

Zekiel closed his bedroom door softly and let out a heavy breath while resting beside it. With closed eyes he tried to distract himself from the despair that he was feeling, so intense that he felt it was consuming him. At only twenty years old this was the worst pain he had ever faced in his life. He began pacing back and forth around his room and fought endlessly with himself in his mind. His parents already attempted to talk to him to offer any kind of support they could, but he refused to open up. It was hard for him to even open up to his own self. He passed by the window and opened up his old and unclean curtains. A wintry breeze fell over him as he watched clouds creep slowly across the sky.

One phone call had changed his entire life. It had altered not only what he felt, but every single thing that he saw around him. The weight of emotion burdening him was so heavy that he could hardly breathe. He was lightheaded, nauseous, and his vision became blurry. His thoughts were unstable and uncontrollable as they taunted him repeatedly. *Was what happened all his fault? Could he have stopped her from going to visit her friend at all? Why did he let her go?* There were too many unanswered questions for him to handle. He opened the glass window and peered over the edge. He lived high up in an apartment complex many floors from the street below. Zekiel fought off the urge to jump. He told himself that time and rest was what he needed to get through the suffering. He made his way over to the messy mattress in the corner of his room to lie down and sat onto it slowly.

He looked straight ahead and caught his reflection in the mirror placed across from him. He examined himself carefully: the way his blonde hair messily pointed off into different directions, how crooked his nose was, and he studied what he thought to be the unattractive qualities of himself he would give anything to change. All he could see was how broken he seemed to be and obsessed over the things he believed he needed to fix, not the kind that can be saved, but the type that's ruined beyond repair and should be tossed away. He stood up and went back over to the window and placed his left leg over the edge.

Zekiel looked at the busy street under him that was teeming with life. Right before he went to shift his entire weight outwards, he began to wonder what this would solve. Maybe he would escape all the misery in his heart, but he started contemplating who would be hurt the most by his death. He didn't feel as though his parents loved or even remotely cared for him. With no siblings and few friends, he almost felt as if his fall would go completely unnoticed. *What about Saige?* The thought of what it would do to her made him feel even worse than he already did. Zekiel couldn't remember a time in his life when he didn't know Saige. She consistently supported him and he could confide in her when the worst of times would bring challenges. "Storms will eventually subside..." she always reminded him, "They might pass quickly and sometimes they feel like they will never pass at all. Don't forget that they will pass."

He decided to back down with the thought of her in his mind and wanted nothing more than to talk to her at that moment. Zekiel glanced at his clock–2:37 a.m. in bright red glared back at him. Only an hour ago he was asleep in a far better place than he was in that moment. The world was simpler and far less cruel in his dreams.

The phone call he received from his girlfriend's parents had changed him forever. He never stopped feeling the pain of what he had lost. For comfort he pulled up the only contact that he felt he could trust from his phone.

"Can I meet you outside? I really need to come see you." he stated.

"What's wrong? Are you hurt?" She didn't hesitate with her next words. "Yes, I'll meet you there."

"I'm on my way now."

Zekiel put on warmer clothes and headed over to Saige's house, which was located only a few blocks away from where he lived. As he went down the sidewalk, he remembered some of the memories he shared with her on this block as they grew up together. He felt a small amount of warmth inside of him upon having these thoughts, which he was indescribably grateful for.

He stepped up onto her porch and saw her resting on the door frame already waiting for him.

"Zeek." She was the only person who shortened his name and he didn't mind because it made him feel at home. "What's wrong?"

"I'm sorry I'm waking you up at three in the morning."

"Don't be. You know I'm here to talk to you whenever you need it. What's going on?" She walked towards him, clutching onto her warm cotton blanket she had wrapped around herself.

"Jasmine got in a car accident a few hours ago on her way back home." He felt his eyes well up with tears and the lump in his throat almost made it impossible for him to swallow. "She didn't make it."

Saige fell into his arms and buried her face into his chest. Neither spoke for a while as they mourned in silence.

Present

"We need to get out of here before one of us is next." Omar broke the tension in the air.

I looked over at Saige who was wiping her eyes and put my arm around her gently.

"I'll get us out of here." I tried to tell her as convincingly as I could. Saying those words out loud helped ease the tension and I needed to hear them too.

Since we were heading upwards and away from the ocean, we had to climb back up the face of a cliff we came down. I instructed Saige to go in front me. I needed to be there to catch her if she fell. With trust for me in her eyes, she got onto the first rock that looked sturdy enough to balance on. I tried to be strong for her in the turn of events we were experiencing. The only problem was that I didn't really know how to be that way for her, for anyone actually, and especially not my own self. With furrowed eyebrows and a stoic expression, I tried to cover up the unsteady emotion that followed me everywhere I went. Back at home it was already bad enough... but being in a place I've never known surrounded by new people with their own set of problems was daunting for me. I didn't want to let Saige down or accidentally allow anything bad happen to a friend that was as great as her.

As she grabbed onto a rock, she turned around and her eyes met mine. I nodded, motioning for her to keep moving forwards. I wasn't in the mood to talk. She smiled as she continued–clearly not catching that I was on the verge of a panic attack. *Having long hair that covers up my face is great.* I let a few more strands fall in front of my eyes and looked through them while I followed after Saige. I could feel heaviness in the air. *Why does it feel like there's something she is not telling me?*

After a challenging climb, we noticed a cave opening on the side of a hill past the wheat field that we had decided to head to.

"None of you worry," Anon placed both his hands out. "I will go in first and check everything again for all of you."

"You know you didn't have to last time, you volunteered yourself." Omar reminded him.

He placed his hand on Omar's shoulder. "I think you're recalling what happened at the bunker incorrectly. If you'll all excuse me now, I have some looking around to do." He smiled and shined a flashlight that he took from the bunker in front of him again as he ventured inside of the cave.

"I'm saying this because I know we're all thinking it." Zayika spoke, "Anon is really annoying."

"I can hear you still!" his voice echoed back at us. "It's also empty in here. We should take some time to reorganize our stuff and make sure it's split up between all of us."

I went in after him with Saige still close by me. Zayika and Omar were in front of us. "Oh, so now you care about fairness?" Zayika continued on. "Says the same guy who literally took about sixty percent of what was in the bunker for himself."

"What? I gave some of it away to you guys. Besides, I'm sort of the leader here. I obviously have a large say over things."

"Since when were you elected leader?" she snorted.

"I've been one basically since the moment we got here. Who's been stepping up to make the risky decisions?"

"Not just you." She rolled her eyes at him.

"Alright guys, since we can actually rest for a while, let's relax." I helped Saige sit down and gave her the sweater I was wearing. "Try not to get too cold."

We laid all of our bandages, canned and boxed foods, water bottles, and more miscellaneous things we had been carrying. We tried to split up our belongings the best that we could. We all caught our breaths and huddled closely together to try and provide warmth for one another. We spent time going around in a circle sharing things about ourselves.

"So how long have you two been in a relationship?" Anon nodded his head in the direction of Saige and me.

We both exchanged looks and shook our heads. "We aren't." I told him.

"Really? Oh wow. Sorry, I just picked up those vibes, you know?" He smirked as the two of us awkwardly gave him half smiles.

I felt Saige grip along my arm gently as she tucked a strand of her hair behind an ear. "We've known each for a really long time. Zekiel and I have always been close."

"You guys arrived here together?"

"We woke up near one another, yes." I replied. For some reason I never thought about how we were the only two who had already met before we got to the planet. "I don't know why."

"Wow, that's interesting. I wish the same happened for me with at least one of my friends... then I wouldn't feel as lonely." Anon looked almost instantly as if he regretted saying that. "I mean no offense to you all! Not that you aren't good company, it would just be nice to have something or someone from home close you know?"

We all agreed with him by nodding heads.

"You two are lucky." He stated.

Saige smiled and softly pulled me closer to her. "We are."

As we continued talking, we began to hear the faint sound of footsteps approaching our cave. I put my finger up to my mouth to make sure everyone stayed silent until whatever it was hopefully passed. It didn't pass... it kept coming closer. We had backed up and cornered our own selves into an area we couldn't easily escape from. With no weapons we were unable to fight back what was arriving at any moment. With bated breaths we stood attentively. A man appeared at the entrance way with skin that looked almost as if it was completely made of tree bark. He had leafy green hair pulled into a ponytail and held what looked to be a gun that was assembled out of pieces of nature. A lady who was very similar in her appearance came up behind him and made direct eye contact with us.

"We caught up to them." she spoke into a device which was also was created from a variety of glowing branches and stones.

"There's more than we expected." he said to her and she shook her head dramatically.

"We'll only take one, I think that's all we need."

"Which do you think would be the best one?"

"How about the man with the long hair? His build will come in handy."

"Good idea." His eyes locked onto me. "You... you're coming with us!"

I thought it was best to not try to fight back, I didn't have the energy or willpower to, so I walked over to where they were. "Where are you taking me?"

"Your new home." The lady replied. She tore off some of the thick vines growing out of her arm and tied my hands behind my back. "Thank you for being one of the few to not make this difficult on us."

"Wait!" Saige panicked. "You can't do this! You can't take him! Pick me instead! I'll go." She rushed forwards.

The man yanked me out of the cave roughly with his companion close by as we walked away. "We need him."

"Then take me too!" Saige cried out and they also secured her arms together.

CHAPTER FOUR: TRANSFORMATIONAL LEADERSHIP

Anon

Present

"This can't be happening." With both of my hands resting on my head, I began pacing around. There were only three of us left. *How long would it be until we were taken next?* My heart thumped heavily in my chest as my breathing became out of control.

I was in utter disbelief at the mess that was ensuing. One by one each of us were being kidnapped, pried away from each other and taken to parts of the planet we had never seen before. Zekiel was chosen by those who looked like they belonged to the jungle and Saige had decided to let herself be taken by them too. *She is more loyal than a lot of people.* It seemed as though no matter what happened... she would remain near Zekiel. It had been a while since I had companionship and I really missed it. I longed to feel important to someone else. I also wanted to inspire others, especially during these times. I liked the group of us that had banded together. Unfortunately, it looked as though we all would be trapped no matter where we ran off to or the places we could try to hide in. *If only that bunker had worked out for us… Who is the man living there?*

Being in the cave that we were in started to bring back memories of the dimly lit bunker and its concrete walls. At least there was food and supplies to help us get along, but now it seemed as though there was no direction for us to take to advance on and be rescued so we could return home. *What will happen to Amira, Zekiel, and Saige?* I felt like I had let them down. I found myself biting into my lip a bit too hard and I drew some blood at the side of my mouth. As I wiped it away, I saw Omar giving me a distressed look.

"Anon!" Omar swung around at me. "Are you alright?"

I shook my head and tried to act as calm as possible. "It's nothing. I'm fine so don't worry about me."

Zayika came over and patted my back roughly as I leaned down onto my shaking kneecaps. "Ugh, just calm down, I think I have some water left in my pack. Try to hold yourself together while I grab it."

What are we going to do? What is happening? Who were the people that took two of the only people we had left with us? So many questions had begun arising which made my mind turn foggy. *What are they going to do to Saige and Zekiel? What if I'm the last one left?*

"The two of you seem so calm. I mean, what if they die?" My thoughts felt irrational and incoherent. "What if they are already dead?"

I was then handed a partially full water bottle from Zayika. "I actually don't think they're going to die."

The two of us focused on her with confused looks. That possibility hadn't seemed to have completely crossed my mind. Maybe they were alive…. Maybe. *How?*

She took our silent response as an invitation to elaborate. "Don't you think if they wanted us dead they would've killed us when they found us? You don't think them pointing out that they only needed one person is a clue to something that we don't know about?"

"You really think that Amira made that dive down into the water out alive?" Omar scoffed and crossed his arms as he always did. "Believe me I'm a wishful thinker but I don't–"

"Listen. It could be a possibility, okay? Clearly that woman who took her lives down there somehow. She wasn't fully human."

"Who knows. I just don't want to get my hopes up." Thankfully my breathing pattern was returning to normal as I regained my composure.

"Let's follow them and see where they're taking Saige and Zekiel. It hasn't been long and we could probably keep enough distance between them so they don't notice us." Zayika lit up with a small spark of vicious excitement as she told us this.

"Why not? I'd rather die trying to find them instead of dying while sitting around feeling sorry for ourselves." I knew I needed to step up and get my head clear.

Omar nodded as he gathered his things. "I agree. Let's head out." We made our way in the direction of their footprints and he took an interest in what happened to me back at the cave, "Anon, are you sure you're doing alright now?"

"Yeah." I responded.

"Because you weren't a few minutes ago."

"I got over it." I lied to him.

"Okay. I haven't. I still feel shook up inside."

"Then how'd you manage to look so relaxed?" I asked Omar.

"You couldn't see the fear in your eyes like I could. I was just trying my best to not panic too. If I also lost it then I would've only made things worse. Believe me. I don't know how Zayika took all of that so well, it's like it didn't even phase her."

We were both silent for a while.

I finally found something to say. "All of this has been hard. I've dealt with this quite a bit in my life."

"Waking up on strange planets? Wow, because this is actually a first for me." Omar laughed as he watched Zayika. She was striding ahead of us in a determined walk.

I wasn't in the mood for joking around. "No. Groups falling apart and people disappearing. Getting close to people is a waste of time when it's so temporary... you're just left feeling empty."

"Seems like you need a good friend. So what's your story?"

"My 'story'?"

"Yeah, everyone has one." Omar said matter-of-factly.

"It's nothing spectacular. Back at home I had many things decided for me. Not just by my parents, but also my friends. I felt pressure constantly to please all of them. I tried to but that meant I was pulled in many different directions. You can't please everyone; you can try, but you just end up getting someone else upset with what you do. I guess everything seemed to begin really falling apart once my parents got divorced."

"...I'm sorry to hear that."

"You don't have to be sorry. It wasn't your fault. I think it was mine."

Four Years Before

Class had just finished as Anon gathered his college textbooks underneath his arm. It had been a long day, each minute had felt like an entire hour, and all the work he would do seemed pointless to him. He believed there was so much time in the world and that all he was doing was wasting it by sitting idly in a classroom. He would daydream of traveling the world and learning the lessons that school was trying to teach him by escaping to live his life–not by listening to a professor speak in an assigned seating spot. The rest of the class started heading out of the doorway when he caught a glimpse of one of his classmates looking at him from across the room. She gave him a welcoming smile and then began following behind everyone else. He had never met her before, but really wanted to. She was in one of his other classes and he didn't ever seem to find the chance to talk to her. This was the last period for the day, so he made his way over to see if the time was right.

"Hey." He stepped around some desks and chairs to get closer to her. "I'm Anon."

She moved out of the way to shake his hand. "I'm Estrella."

"It's nice to finally meet you."

She had caught the subtle hint in his words. "You too."

He wasn't sure what to say next. He never thought he'd actually get as far as he did.

"Can I walk you out?"

"Sure."

Everyone else in the room besides their teacher was already gone and after waving goodbye to him they went outside.

"So... how old are you? I'm twenty."

"Same age."

"Have you lived here your whole life?" Anon asked.

"No, I actually moved here to attend community college. What about you?"

"Yeah I have. It can get pretty boring. It's nice to meet someone new."

Estrella and Anon found a park bench in front of their school to occupy as they got to know each other and waited for their rides to arrive. Their conversation was going well. Anon tried to learn as much as he could about her, but time wasn't on their side. After a short while, he noticed that his parents had driven into the parking lot so he said goodbye to Estrella. As he approached the handle to the car door, his intuition set off a warning in the way that he felt.

"Hey." Anon spoke as he entered the backseat with his parents both in front of him. Neither said anything. "Is everything alright?"

No one spoke until they had driven a few blocks away from the college. The radio wasn't on like it usually was, only the air conditioner was turned up so that it could cool down the warm day. His mom let out a heavy sigh and glanced into the rearview mirror at him. "No, everything is not alright. Would you like to be the one to tell him what's going on?" She looked distastefully at his father.

"There's no easy way around saying what's the truth here, Anon. We were going to talk when we got home but we might as well get it over with now. Your mother and I are... we're getting a divorce."

Anon felt a lump forming in his throat even though he had already seen that announcement coming for years. He tried to be ready for it, but it actually happening was something he could never truly be prepared for. There had been so many sleepless nights in his household with several memories that took place in the middle of the night. He would lay in bed wide awake listening to the sounds of his parents yelling at each other downstairs for hours. *Why couldn't what was wrong be fixed?*

"Am I allowed to ask why?" He watched out the window, viewing the world as a blur while they sped along winding roads in between grassy hills. Tears formed in his eyes slowly as he bit his lip. He tried to hide his tears from his mother and father.

"Anon." His mother spoke as gently as she could. "We both talked about this for a long time while you were gone and this is a decision we think is the right one to take. The two of us, we just aren't right for one another and I think you know that."

"Then why did you even get married in the first place?" He already knew the answer to his own question. His parents had become pregnant with him when they were young teenagers. They were practically forced into marrying one another by their own parents in order to get any financial or emotional support from them. It almost wasn't their choice to get married–familial pressure had sparked this problem and Anon knew that. "Forget it."

"Look, I know you're upset, but... this is a little bit harder on us than you."

He scoffed. "Really? I've had to put up with you two hating each other and fighting nonstop for twenty years. Neither of you have once made me feel like I'm loved by you. I know it was my fault that you two got together, okay? I already know that I'm a mistake. I'm going for a walk." He opened his car door as they approached a stop light and stepped outside into the middle of traffic.

"Anon, where are you going?" his mother yelled out of her window.

Present

The three of us didn't know how long we had been traveling through the humid day. We kept our distance from the two strangers that took Saige and Zekiel, but we followed close enough so that they wouldn't notice us. We had all grown tired, quiet, and communicated with one another through glances and hand gestures as we reached our next destination.

"Look over here." Omar glanced down below at the ground. "Are these vines that are growing?"

"Seems like it." I replied.

We were venturing into the jungle. It was clear that we needed to watch where we were stepping. *Hopefully there are no hidden creatures or traps here.* I was mindful of where I placed my feet and hands to guide myself through the vegetation. Some of the dirt below us was damp and I could tell that my shoes were muddy.

"If either of you notice any pillars of smoke from off in the distance, make sure you let me know." I started to joke. "You know, in case there are others we don't know about."

"Obviously there are others here, Anon, we are following them right now." Zayika replied dryly.

I sighed. "Oh come on, don't tell me you don't know what I'm talking about."

"It's alright dude. I'll keep a lookout for the others only if you make sure there isn't a smoke monster in the jungle with us." Omar jumped in.

"Thank you! Finally someone who gets it. Let's be best friends." I smiled.

"Let's try not talking for a while." Zayika ended the short-lived interaction.

Far up ahead I could see Saige and Zekiel still being led by the woman and man who had appeared at the cave. They seemed to have their hands gripped on their shoulders to guide them along the way. *Thankfully our friends haven't been hurt.* My mind started to wander as I looked at Omar and Zayika who were next to me. *At least I have these two in my corner.* Omar's body language was making him seem guarded. Ever since I had met him, I noticed that he crossed his arms constantly. It seemed almost as if he felt that doing so would protect him from the dangers in the world, like others' harsh words that seemed to get under his skin. Zayika strode with her arms at her side and kept a cold expression on her face. Her eye color was striking and her words with whatever was behind them made her intimidating and mysterious to a certain degree. She had really long silver and purple hair that was wavy at the tips and would bounce off of her shoulders as she moved around. I had a strange feeling that, like her hair, there was another side to her—but she wasn't letting us see it.

"What is it you're staring at?" she asked sharply after noticing that I had been looking in her direction.

"Nothing." I kept my answer brief, slightly startled that she had singled me out yet again.

"I guess we can start cutting off some distance from them now that we are well covered. It's kind of hard to see." Zayika pushed at branches that were in front of her.

"Is that some kind of treehouse?" I jogged towards the direction we were being led to and pointed towards their grounds.

I spotted some cover in front of a large boulder near the building that the four in front of us were going into. What was ahead had the appearance of an overgrown house of plants made out of abandoned and earthy materials.

Zayika tried to step past us as Omar, who was kneeling, grabbed a hold of her ankle. "What are you doing?" he asked.

"Don't touch me." She kicked him with her other leg. "I'm getting a closer look."

As it came into view, we saw that the building was quite large. Zayika noticed Saige and Zekiel in a crowd of people who closely resembled the ones that took them away. Some had crowns that were made out of sharpened and shaped wood, oaky bark where normal skin would be, and moss for hair.

Zayika looked down at Omar and me. "I don't know how we're going to get them. You both need to see this."

"How are we going to get in?" I asked, huddled next to them. "I'm pretty sure those are guards." I pointed in the direction of two people dressed in heavy looking metal armor.

"We'll have to be stealthy then." Omar said nervously.

Zayika grinned at the sound of Omar's words. "I have an idea. Let's get ourselves covered in dirt and plants like they are. If we're disguised, how are they going to see a difference?"

I was impressed. It seemed like Zayika had a decent plan for the first time since I met her instead of just a snarky remark. "That might actually work."

We readied ourselves by rolling around onto the ground beneath us. We pulled vines and leaves from nearby trees and tucked them into our hair and branches under our shirts and pants. After what felt like a few minutes, we were ready enough to venture out closer to Saige and Zekiel.

"Don't act suspicious." I instructed them both.

"How do you 'act suspicious'?" Omar spoke while wiping dirt away from his lips with a repulsed look on his face.

"I don't know. Try your best to blend in."

I led the way for them as we walked over to the building. Some of the people we saw had passed right by us without recognizing us as intruders. Zayika's plan was actually working. *Am I irritated that I didn't think of it first? Maybe.*

Zayika stepped ahead and put her arm in front of my chest. "Slow down. We have to think this through carefully."

"What is there to stand here and talk about? Let's just go for it." Omar grew impatient... as he normally did. "We're wasting time and possibly daylight. Let's get them and get out of here."

She rolled her eyes and shrugged. "Alright then, keep moving. Stay close to the right near the wall. Keep your faces low and don't talk to any of them for any reason at all."

We kept to the plan quite effectively for as long as it took to get past half of the building. We were careful to not draw any attention to ourselves and treaded carefully with our steps to not kick up dirt below us. Off to my left I noticed what looked to be a large crate full of weapons.

"Guys hold on. We need to get some of those." I said in a low whisper.

I caught their attention and they agreed with my suggestion so we wandered off towards the gear box as relaxed as we could seem. No one was around or guarding it at the time so we assumed we would be safe. We were wrong of course. When I picked up the weapon closest to me on top, a hefty axe with a wooden handle and freshly sharpened blade, I had the feeling I was being watched. Someone other than my new friends was looking at me. I knew it. I paid attention to my peripheral vision and that's when I saw who–or what–it was. Someone was leaning onto a tree nearby. I could only see half of them, but two small bright green wings behind them stood out to me. We made eye contact for one second and in the next he was already scurrying towards me.

"I'm Gebu!" a high-pitched and squeaky voice proclaimed. "You never should have come here!"

I don't remember what I was going to yell out in return because he had already sprung up into the air and knocked me down to the ground. My breath escaped my lungs painfully. Unfortunately, the axe I had taken fell off to the side and out of my reach. Zayika jumped behind him and grabbed the first weapon she could get a hold of. What she thought was a sword turned out to be nothing at all, there was no blade–only an empty handle.

She cried out in disbelief, "Where did it go?"

"What are you doing?" One of the nature-like people screamed at her. "Just create it!"

I was then smacked squarely in the face by the man with wings on top of me.

"What are you talking about?" she said in a growing panic.

"Wait... you all aren't one of us! We have intruders!" The person who spoke this put her hands out in front of her. I could hardly see what she did next, but I could've sworn she actually crafted a gun from parts of nature around her. "We also told you to leave us alone Gebu!" She aimed and took a shot at my attacker. He dodged the bullet and picked me up while flying into the air.

"Someone stop him!" I heard Omar yell.

"I shall be the chosen one! I shall wish for endless riches for my riches!" I heard another gun shot as Gebu spoke to himself and held onto me tightly. This time the shot had apparently grazed him since he wailed out in pain at a small tear in his wing. His grip on me loosened as we both started plummeting back towards the ground. I felt my heart sink during the fall until I was caught in some sort of netting. Another one of the tree people had created it somehow. I was reminded of the woman at the ocean who had previously wrapped material around me from the palm of her hand when Amira was being captured.

"You all are intruders!" one of them reiterated.

I looked to see what had happened to Gebu. He was motionless on the ground in the middle of a crowd that had formed around him. Zayika and Omar ran over to me and helped me out of the net.

"Someone help me!" Gebu stated dramatically, throwing a hand up to his forehead with his wispy hair flowing in the wind. "It isn't my time. I'm destined to win this!"

"Gebu, it's just a little cut. You'll be fine. How many times do we need to tell you to stop coming here and bothering us? You don't even have any weapons. You couldn't hurt a bumble bee even if you were paid to." the woman who had shot the bullet told him.

"How dare you make such emotionally damaging assumptions of my bravery?" Gebu remained lying sprawled out on the ground.

"Your wings aren't even larger than those of a bumble bee." Everyone started laughing at him mockingly.

"How dare you insult me again? I am one of the most important members of the sky above! My wings are no match for your vines and dirt!"

"Are you serious? You just insulted your own self!" One of the other members said while folding over in laughter. "Now go back to your cotton candy castle residing up in the sky so us adults can fight amongst one another and handle the real stuff!"

Everyone's attention shifted back to us. Omar, Zayika, and I were cornered. I attempted to put my hands up in some sort of sign of surrender, but it didn't seem to matter to them. I took a deep breath and tried to prepare myself for a bullet or knife to go through me. Instinctively I closed my eyes. I waited but nothing happened. I looked around and noticed that everyone wasn't staring at our faces anymore, but at our feet. It was then I started to feel the ground below me quake as if it was falling apart. They all quickly shuffled backwards and away from us.

"What's going on?" I asked.

No one answered but instead all stood in shock.

One of the tree-like people turned to a man behind her and tapped his shoulder to get his attention. "This is incredible. I've never actually seen anyone go through the process of being taken away."

"You think this is a sight to see? How about someone actually becoming morphed?" They replied eagerly.

"No way. You've seen that?"

"Yeah, I don't know how most of the people who go through it survive. I can't believe we did."

"We must be the strong ones."

"Let's just hope these three aren't weak like the unfortunate."

"You're wrong, we need them to be. That way they'll be easier to kill."

"That's true."

I wasn't sure if I should've been more concerned with what they were saying or the ground that was cracking beneath our feet. The foundation where we stood began to rise up into the air and carried the three of us towards the sky. We watched in terror as everyone below kept shrinking until they faded from our view. As we continued upwards, I lost a lot of feeling in my legs and almost tumbled over the edge. Thankfully Zayika had a quick reaction time and caught me swiftly.

"Hang onto me." she said loudly over the sound of the earthquake below us.

"I can't handle heights, guys!" Omar had his eyes closed.

Zayika took the sleeve of his jacket in her free hand. "Without me you two would probably already be dead."

"I don't think that matters now!" My stomach felt like a knot as I really saw how high we were getting. I looked up and noticed a layer of scattered clouds that looked unnaturally solid, like we wouldn't even be able to pass through them. "I wonder what will happen if we hit that?"

"We're going to find out!" Omar wailed loudly.

The platform we were on kept hurtling towards the thick mysterious cloudy substance without slowing down. We were only seconds away from it. We braced ourselves in unison for some sort of impact at any moment but there was none. After speeding through what we thought would kill us, we were suddenly in the midst of a breathtaking floating city. I was in awe. More platforms arose to form a path for us to get to the other side. Only one of us could go at a time and we looked at each other to see who would take the first leap–I was the first to speak up.

"I can do it." I slowly glanced over the edge of where I stood and realized just how far I would have to jump in order to make it. I decided it was better to not build suspense for myself, so I stepped back a few steps and got ready to sprint. *Hopefully they are somewhat impressed by this...*

"Wait!" Zayika said quickly. "I didn't even see this on here before! Grappling hooks and strings."

I didn't believe her words at first, but I looked in her hands and saw that she was right. Equipment that had blended in with the colors of the ground was there for us to use.

"Okay so, these are a little bit helpful." I smiled and laughed as I dug the first hook into our platform and tied the string into it carefully. "It's now or never, right? I'll see you guys on the other side."

When I sprung off the edge time felt almost as if it stood still in that moment between the two points. I was gripping onto the rope so tightly that I began losing feeling in my fingers but I ended up making it. *Barely.*

"Anon, are you alright?" Omar asked.

I didn't blame him for being concerned since I was just barely hanging on the edge that I had flung towards. "I'm amazing." I grunted as I pulled myself onto the surface.

Zayika and, by some miracle, Omar followed after and we eventually made it to the entrance of the floating city at which we had arrived.

"We're going to go in there?" Omar crossed his arms judgmentally.

"Well I know that I'm going to. If you'd rather head back down and try to not get smacked by Gebu that's your choice, I won't judge you, but I personally would love to not plummet to my death today." I gave him a pat on his shoulder as I attempted to open the large silver gate. I must have triggered some sort of alarm because a loud booming noise began to ring out through the entire sky.

"Who is at this gate?" We heard.

"I'm Anon." I threw my hands up. "I'm with my, uh, friends Zayika and Omar. We aren't meaning to cause any harm here."

"We've been waiting for you. Come in."

The gate began opening and we made our way inside.

Two Years Before

The car rumbled on the side of the road next to a row of empty shops. Anon processed the words that were just spoken to him as thoroughly as he could.

"So, that's it?" Anon asked Estrella. "You're going to give up on me?"

The two had been dating for a while after his parent's divorce and throughout the previous months Anon had felt a change in the way she acted towards him.

She hit her hand against the horn, jolting slightly as she did so. "Don't look at it that way. Why would you word it like that? I just have a stronger connection with a different guy, okay? I have felt this way for months. Don't act like the victim here because I can't help how I feel Anon."

Rain fell slowly down the passenger window. Anon watched the droplets race each other as warm air from the car blew his strands of hair around. "I have been trying to make this relationship work for months. Why didn't you just tell me that you found someone else sooner? You are always so quiet. Now you decide to finally speak up and this is what you say?"

"It's unfair to say that I am 'always' silent. There's a lot that can be heard in silence. It's not my fault that you were so busy with your parent's divorce, and whatever else, that you put me in the background."

"Estrella, I'm sorry that you feel I didn't prioritize you or this relationship, but I really needed to work through my emotions. Please just stay with me so we can figure this out."

"We can't!" Lightning struck that was accompanied by thunder. Estrella's eyes grew wider as she looked in Anon's direction. He had never seen her like this before. The car was dim with only the front panel lights and the whites of her eyes glowing solemnly. "I don't want this to be messy, our separation, but I feel like we are fighting for something that does not make any sense and will go nowhere."

He rolled his shoulders and stretched his legs outwards. Anon thought carefully about the words he had just heard. "You really don't think we can make this work?"

"Listen, I just feel like some things are supposed to fall apart. What profound stories are there that don't have some extent of tragedy to them? I think that it's a part of life's seasons. I have no doubt that later on you will find a better companion than me, maybe you aren't meant to have a partner at all, go find that out. Do yourself a favor and find your strength."

Anon took that last sentence as his exit cue. Every footstep he took from then on felt heavy as he walked across the street. The fog in the sky paired with the tears in his eyes made it too difficult to see where he was going. He could hear Estrella's voice calling after him, but it didn't matter anymore, because he didn't matter anymore to her. Chills swept over him as he pulled his rain covered jean jacket in tighter. Anon had been struck by lightning that he didn't see coming. Forever in his veins and heart would be the color blue.

Present

I was locked into a floating glass cylinder. I looked at who was in the room with me and noticed two men who seemed as if they were born out of the sky itself. Their skin was bright and one even had small floating clouds that followed him around as he walked. One of them had put both of his arms out in front of him and the whole room began spinning in one swift motion. It was like we were inside of a tornado as he controlled the air since he made it swirl and rush around. Every item that was around us was flying rapidly too as he and the other stranger were standing still and watching me anxiously. I gave them a concerned look, wondering what they were waiting for. Before I could even blink, it had started.

An unbearable amount of searing pain began to fill my body. From limb to limb I felt like I was being torn apart and shredded up. I gasped for air as I felt the cage I was in beginning to shrink around me... *maybe my body is getting larger?* My eyes were forcefully closed in reaction to the striking sounds of thunder and lightning that I could hear. This went on for some time while I tried to make sense of what was happening. I finally gained enough courage to open my eyes. I watched as lightning stung through my veins like it replaced the warm blood that once filled them. I winced in horror as I could feel every part of myself changing. The only thought I remembered having in that moment was me thinking to my own self: *will I ever be the same after this?*

CHAPTER FIVE: INTRUSION

Saige

Present

Every part of my body was aching and sore. I had no idea what happened to me. After Anon, Omar, and Zayika were taken up into the air, the two strangers who captured Zekiel and me knocked us unconscious in one of their rooms. As I drifted back into reality... I saw fading leaves in front of my eyes that I pulled at until I realized that they were a part of my hair. This led me to wonder how different I looked since they had clearly changed my appearance too.

I heard someone in another room say, "She's been morphed successfully." Something inexplicably felt different within me. When I became more aware of my surroundings I noticed that the room was misty. I looked down at what I was wearing and was shocked at what I found. Vines in jagged patterns were embedded into my arms, legs... basically everywhere on my body. I attempted to pull them out of my skin, but I couldn't because leaves were growing there too.

My uneasiness grew stronger. *What did they do to me?* I sat up off of the rock bed they had me on and went over to the only mirror on the wall to get a closer look. They somehow made my body faintly transparent so I could see through my skin, which made it feel as though it was crawling! I was actually able to see every single one of my veins that had the appearance of small intricate branches. I could see a substance pumping through them and my whole body had a green luminous appearance. I felt like I had become a monster. I heard footsteps approaching and spun to see who it was. Zekiel, now also morphed, came towards me looking as shocked as I did.

"Zeek!" I bolted into his arms and held him close. Our embrace was short lived once I felt how unnaturally stiff his hug was. "Are you okay?" I asked as I stepped back. My expression changed quickly.

"What? Am I not pretty anymore?" He laughed and I was glad to hear jokes coming from him.

"Your skin. You're... it's... tree bark?" I took his arm in my hand and ran my fingertips along the bumpy and rough wood where his smooth skin used to be. There were even plants that had started to grow out of small indents in his chest. Parts of the clothes we both had on when we got morphed were ruined and tattered, the holes and wear in them showed the unbelievable changes that we had just gone through.

"This isn't that noticeable, right?" Zekiel kept laughing as I stood there, still shocked and almost unable to speak. "Enough about me. Look at what they did to you."

"I already have." I let out a deep sigh as I tried to avoid thinking about myself. "I'm trying to ignore this as much as I can honestly."

"It's not that bad. At least we are still alive."

He always made me smile.

"Yes, we're safe and that's what matters most."

We then heard a movement in the hallway nearby.

"I'm glad to see you're both still alive. I had a feeling that you two would be, you seemed like some of the stronger ones from in the cave." I saw the man that ruined us enter the room.

"We demand answers from you! What did you do? What is it that you want from us?" Zekiel held me back by my arm.

"I'm glad you're so eager to learn. Truly, this might really be a fun experience if you keep an open mind. We want you to represent your new people proudly as you fight for this faction's victory."

"What faction?"

"I forgot how much you will need to learn in order to get started. My name is Fabian." He gestured for us to follow him as we went down a corridor. He motioned all around and gave us a tour of what I assumed would be our living space... I didn't want to call it a home. "Welcome to the Land Dwellers faction. We are one of the only three that exist on this planet with our rivals being the Oceanic Guardians and the Over Grounds. We believe in being in tune with nature as well as using its powerful forces to our ultimate advantage in combat. We focus boldly on charging courageously in the battlefield. Once someone appears here on the hills it becomes first come first serve with faction gets to find and recruit that individual to be morphed into our groups."

"Listen to me," I struggled to gain enough confidence to speak up for Zekiel and myself. "We did not ask for this! I demand you change us back to the way we were and send us back to where we came from!"

Instead of an apologetic reaction or threatening look from Fabian that I was waiting for, he laughed at me. I could tell he genuinely was amused.

"While I really do admire the ambition that you possess, you need to realize that you can't get what you want. You'll have to live with that and face this challenge that's before you."

My world began spinning and my lip trembled. Zekiel instinctively looped his rough arm underneath mine to calm me down and grabbed my hand.

"Let us go now." His voice spoke in a way that I never had heard before. His words made the room rumble.

Fabian tossed his hands upwards. "This type of passion is exactly what we need in our faction! I will count my lucky stars tonight that we found you before the others did."

"I said now!" Zekiel yelled and jumped forward. I let out a small shriek as a flame found its way through his palm that was holding onto mine. "What did you do to us?" Terror filled his lungs as he looked at me holding onto the minor injury that he inflicted.

"You were on fire!" I told him as he tried to piece together what he had just accidentally done to me.

"If you are wise, you will not turn against me." Fabian seemed unfazed by what just happened and warned both of us. "If you are wise, you will learn what each of your bodies do. Clearly you need to practice honing it in and being more in tune with it. You each have one single power. If you think with your mind and not your heart you will win this game alongside your new kind. The two of you seem to operate based on emotions and not logic; the way you both think is very unfortunate. You don't know the creatures that are out there and the pain you will face. You seem to have a solid bond which the old me would have admired, but now I think that not being rational about your circumstances and hopes of survival is one of the most foolish things that you can do. Fight for your faction, or fight for your feelings, death is promised either way. The opening ceremony will be coming up soon. The rest of your questions will be answered then." He left us alone.

"I will get us out of here. I will. I promise." Zekiel fought back tears. "I'm sorry I hurt you. I'm hurting so badly right now. Saige–I don't know what to do."

Three Years Before

"Why are you taking me here?" Zekiel asked Saige as they pulled into a parking spot near the entryway of a park near their houses.

"Because you need to get out of your room. Feeling the sun on your skin should help." She gave him a kind look while turning her car off. With her hand placed on his, she gripped his fingers tightly. "Also because I miss you and we have not been spending enough time together. So if you don't want to go to the park, then please do it for me."

Zekiel rubbed the back of his neck, "You've always had a way with words."

"Is that a smile I see?"

"Of course it isn't. I haven't smiled for two years. Not since that night."

"We'll have to change that. I know I'm two years younger than you, but that doesn't mean I don't know what's good for you."

Both of them set off down the park's main pathway. They passed several growing trees and content visitors conversing with one another while enjoying the soothing summer weather.

Saige swayed their linked arms through the air. "Where do you see yourself a few years from now?"

Zekiel stared at his shoes and avoided eye contact. "I don't know Saige. I can't think right now about the future because I see no light in it."

"It doesn't have to be that way. Look, I do believe that time is capable of healing wounds."

"Everyone says that Saige, but it's been two years now and I don't feel any different. It's like I live in a world where time doesn't exist anymore."

Suddenly a woman approached Zekiel and Saige with her phone in her hand, set to camera mode. "Would you guys mind taking a photo of my husband and me please? I'm sorry to have interrupted your conversation."

Zekiel shrugged and Saige nodded enthusiastically. Saige took the stranger's phone and took a few photos for them posing side by side near a bed of flowers. They were thanked for their time and the two continued walking towards the closest bench. The physical space between the two friends felt heavy, as if there were words that were supposed to be said that were not being spoken.

"Before Jasmine died, I don't think I understood the impact of death." Zekiel sat down across from Saige.

"Oh. What do you mean by that?"

"I didn't fully realize just how serious it is. We all know we will die someday. We read stories about death and attempt to compensate with it by telling jokes sometimes, but I never felt the pain it truly brings into my life until Jasmine lost hers. We need to look out for one another. Life is very fragile."

Present

Zekiel and I decided that we should discover as much information about what was going on as we could before the opening ceremony. I was so thankful to not be alone in the turn of events that took place. Having Zekiel work together with me for survival was one of the best gifts I was given. I always tried to look out for him, and because of his heart, he was also looking out for me. I watched and admired him as we walked around. The changes taking place were beyond stressful, but I was thankful to have someone I knew I could rely on. As we turned through a few of the building's corners we came across someone we hadn't met. A young woman with gentle eyes greeted us with an outstretched arm. She had no hesitation presenting a warm welcome.

"You must be the new members! I'm really excited to meet you both. I've already heard some things about you from Fabian." She smiled and shook our hands. "My name is Saylor."

"Nice to meet you." Zekiel responded. "Do you mind telling us what is going on here? I'm sure that's a question you get often?"

"Yes, definitely from newcomers. Now our faction is complete though! So long story short, you will hear about everything at the opening ceremony that is coming up soon. What was your morphing experience like? Did it go well? What abilities did you receive? Show me them!"

I didn't step forwards. "I don't know what mine is. I'm still trying to adjust to whatever it is they did to me."

"Well we are definitely going to have to figure that power out!" She seemed so excited. *Why is she acting like all of this is a positive thing?* "Okay so what about you?" Saylor pointed to Zekiel.

"I know that I can produce fire. I did it accidentally earlier in the heat of the moment. That and my skin now is growing bark so... that's really comfortable." He made it obvious when he was being sarcastic.

"Those two things don't physically sound like the best mix. I guess you'll have to be careful with how many flame rounds you make at a time. Letting abilities cool down is extremely important, that's one thing the rest of us have learned so far while testing them out. Be sure that you mindfully cool down before producing too many projectiles in a row." Saylor looked at the tree bark that covered Zekiel's muscular arms.

"So Saylor, what ability do you have?" I asked her. I figured it would be fun to turn the tables around... and take her attention away from Zekiel.

"I can do this." Saylor began crafting a bow and arrow from her arms. I cringed at the shards of wood that pierced out from her pores. "I have to use arrows sparsely though since I can only make a certain amount before needing to take a break. Making weapons is something that only a few of us can do. Why don't we step outside and test out the abilities that you both have?"

We agreed with her and walked onto a patch of stones in the backyard area of the building. The sun was rising steadily and started to bring warmth along with it. Being outdoors in that way reminded me of the days at the park that Zeek and I would have together. There was a slight mist for all of us to try to look through as we spaced out from one another.

"How do you start using your ability?" I broke the silence.

"It's something you have to actively think about in order to use it. Your ability isn't sparked from an internal feeling, it's more of a conscious decision to activate it."

Saylor explained patiently. "At least that's what my friends and I have learned in our time waiting for other members to arrive. We would practice fighting out here, without hurting one another, just trying to discover our capabilities and boundaries."

I nodded my head in acknowledgement of her instructions and looked over at Zekiel. "Is that what it's been like for you?"

"Yes," he responded. "Focus on what you think you're supposed to do." Zekiel's hands started to heat up.

Saylor and I watched as miniscule flames began to appear from within the crevices of both of his palms.

"Make sure you're careful, Zekiel." Saylor warned, "Cooling down is extremely vital to survival. I know I'm repeating myself a lot, but you have to be cautious of how long you've used your abilities or else your flames will begin to engulf your body. The bark and flames aren't going to mix well for you."

Zekiel promptly calmed his body down as his hands returned to normal. "Good point."

"So when you stung my hand earlier... that was intentional then?" I asked Zekiel.

"I forgot that we were holding hands, I'm sorry." He shrugged at me. "Sort of battling my own emotions right now and need to keep my temperature in check."

"I forgive you." I raised my eyebrows. "Don't worry about it. You deserve to vent out problems in whatever way works best. As Saylor said, though, yes–be careful."

I looked at my exposed veins and skin that was much thinner now than it used to be. "This is unsettling."

"Yes it is, Saige, but there has to be a reason why we were chosen to be here." Saylor walked over to me and placed her hands on both of my now sensitive forearms.

"Your heart rate is increasing. What are you thinking about?"

Zekiel started to show discomfort. "What's wrong?"

"I think I'm just trying to process everything that's happening right now. I will try to use my ability." I closed my eyes and attempted to meditate in order to relax my anxiety-filled nerves that were firing off. I started to allow my mind to drift into a blank state.

"We should meditate with you. This will be beneficial for all of us." Saylor and Zekiel closed their eyes with her statement and we all stood silently.

"What in the fresh hell is going on here?" An unfamiliar voice asked seemingly out of nowhere. "Is this what you people do from this group? I came to introduce myself and I find two of you with your eyes closed. Is this what the productivity standard is in this faction? Let me transfer here if it requires no effort."

I opened my eyes to put a face to the voice who was speaking. A man I'd never seen before had arrived; he was tall with pure white wings that were attached to his back. He had straight dark hair which complimented his coarse eyebrows and a cleanly trimmed beard that accentuated his sharp jawline. He wasn't wearing a shirt and squinted at all of us in what looked to be disbelief and an expression of intrigue.

"Who are you?" I heard Saylor ask. "How did you get here?"

"My name's Nero. You aren't very bright, are you? I have wings on my back... can't you see them now that your eyes are open?" He looked enticingly at his medium sized wings. "I bet the two of you have powers also, but not as powerful as mine."

"Wait, 'two' of us? There's three. Saylor, Saige, and me." Zekiel started to look around and point to all of us and noticed that I didn't appear to be there. "Saige, where are you?"

"You guys have an imaginary friend? That's cute I guess." Nero laughed too hard at his own joke.

"I'm right here." I responded until I realized that I must have been blending into what was around me. "I'm not imaginary. You can't see me because... I can blend?"

"Okay so I think I'm getting up to speed. Your team has a chameleon chick - but what are you guys supposed to be?" Nero gave Zekiel and Saylor a sour look. "This dude has tree bark on his arms so what is it that you are responsible for? Crafting paper?"

"We get it Nero. You've made your... shirtless presence known here. Clearly you're a show-off. You don't have to try to act better than the rest of us just because you can fly. I can craft weapons out of thin air. Beat that." Saylor stated playfully.

"Oh believe me I can." Nero began shifting the air around all of us and made it grow forcefully in a matter of seconds. "I can beat you with the thin air itself!"

Nero started to aim his ability around all three of us and pushed us towards one another. I guess at that point I became visible again because he gave me a surprised look.

Zekiel tried to brace his stance on the ground by bending his knees. "Stop using your abilities recklessly!"

Nero kept his arms out in front of him as the air spun faster. "Relax paper maker, it's just a joke. This is what the other girl looks like? I guess I scared her out of hiding." His hollow eyes focused on mine.

"Stop!" Voices emerged from our building as two of our own people from the Land Dweller's faction came sprinting towards us. I had recognized both from earlier in the corridor when Zekiel and I were taken to be morphed.

Nero chuckled and rolled his eyes while deciding to sweep them up into the whirlpool instead of Zekiel, Saylor, and me. "Extra side characters have appeared! This is fun!"

"Put them down! Those are my friends!" Saylor called out. "Are you insane?"

"I'll be whatever you want if you craft whatever I want." Nero winked at her as he started to intensify the wind and flew upwards. "Let's see what we can do with these two wannabe heroes here."

The two were both screaming as they were also lifted into the air. "My lungs!" one of them managed to say.

"You're hurting them!" Saylor started to run towards Nero while creating a metal hook from her right hand; Zekiel and I were stunned that she could make multiple types of weapons. She jumped up and grabbed onto one of Nero's wings with her other hand.

"Let go of me!" Nero tried to shake her off while still holding the two onlookers hostage.

Saylor put her blade onto Nero's wing swiftly as she started to slice through the tender skin that was holding it into place. With the pain that Nero was enduring, he intensified the pressure that he had on the two caught by the air. While pushed up against one another, they both simultaneously exploded from within. Their insides were forced out of them and the wind blew each piece in every direction. We all were covered in their blood and guts as we fixated our eyes on Nero.

"Look at what you did!" Saylor screamed as Nero fell down in pain. She dropped her knife in despair as she looked all over at the scattered remains of her friends, "You killed them!"

"Well... you ruined my wing, you stupid bitch!" Nero cried out.

Nero had blood gushing out of a gaping hole in his back where his wing had previously been attached. He went to reach for the blade that Saylor made and Zekiel created flames in both of his hands. Nero noticed this and sent a shockwave of air towards him which blew the fire out. Saylor was visibly shaking in fear as she remained standing in the same place, not realizing that Nero was now after her.

"Saylor watch out!" I yelled as he successfully grabbed her weapon.

He stomped over behind her and wrapped his arm around her waist as he spoke, "Go die!" He sliced her throat open. Her blood began pouring out and formed a puddle on the ground.

I went invisible and grabbed onto Zekiel as we started to run for our lives. Everything became a blur as I hurriedly put each foot in front of the other, trying to get away as fast as possible. I tried to distract myself from replaying in my head what I had just witnessed as I narrowly dodged tripping over several vines on the ground that were scattered around in tangled knots.

"Where did you both go? Get back here!" I heard Nero call out in a rage as we were sprinting. I then realized that he couldn't see Zekiel either after I had used my ability to disappear. *I guess I can make others go invisible too.*

CHAPTER SIX: UNNERVING REALIZATIONS
Zayika

Present

There were strangers hovering and observing me through glass like I was some sort of an experiment in a lab. I tried to survey my surroundings while a deep ache in my bones and muscles throbbed with each second. My hands shook as I stared at them in disbelief. *Am I dreaming?* While looking at my reflection in the glass, I noticed right away that the freckles covering my skin had changed in shape and color. They were lighter and I could feel specks of warmth from beneath them. I didn't know what ability had been given to me based on those physical changes. The pain I had made me feel more alive and my mind remained unusually at ease despite the circumstances I was under. I felt powerful in an unexplainable and amazing way. *What am I capable of?*

I thought about the people from the ground that had otherworldly powers. *What did I get?* Anticipation washed over me as I looked forward to learning more about myself. Upon hearing nearby murmurs, I realized that I was definitely awake and turned my head to look for Anon and Omar.

"No way." I whispered as my mouth fell open and I hit the glass. "Anon!"

"Zayika I don't know what they did to me." Anon responded hopelessly. "Something started growing, what is it? Can you see?" He shuffled and turned in agony.

"You have wings!" They were entirely coal black and crowded around him. They matched his hair and shirt that had been ripped with pieces missing from it.

Anon's skin seemed as though it had changed too. I could see small specks of blue that were surging within the patterns of veins on his arms. He was clearly in a lot of distress and discomfort as he tried to stay calm in the midst of what was happening. I couldn't believe that this was reality. He was hunching over slightly and tried to wrap an arm around to his back to touch the flesh that had been shredded near his spine where the wings were growing. I didn't have anything happening outwardly that seemed as drastic as what happened to him. *Wait... what about Omar?* I looked over to check on Omar and was somehow in greater disbelief at what I saw.

Omar was sitting in the corner of his cylinder holding his kneecaps close to his chest. His arms trembled as he observed Anon, who was spinning around in anguish. I didn't notice any stark changes to Omar's appearance. He still had the same dark colored curly hair and an expression of worry written all over every inch of his face. Since meeting him there always seemed to be something troubling him or an ailment he had to deal with. So the fact that nothing had happened to him but instead to Anon and me? I wanted answers.

"Why are you… normal?" I asked and he couldn't answer me at first. "Omar! I asked you a question."

He shook his head, "I don't know but I saw the two of you morph. That's what the people here are calling it, 'morphing.' It looked painful."

"What an astute observation." Anon scoffed as he touched his back to find blood dripping from his new wings.

"Sarcasm won't help right now." Omar shot back at him.

"I think he's simply using it as a defense mechanism." I responded in Anon's defense and for Omar's peace of mind. Anon didn't reject my assumption, but instead looked embarrassed by it.

Omar stood up slowly as he looked over his body. "I feel fine and I look the same. Maybe they will be coming back soon to do the same to me. We need to get out of here!" He started to swing punches at the glass cage he was in and I was close to physically trying to shut him up myself.

"Stop!" I responded. "We don't want to make too much noise and draw their attention. We will find a different way to escape."

Anon was staying surprisingly quiet while Omar was panicking. It looked like a switch in his mind had been flipped, like a bit of himself had been stolen. *Why don't I feel bad for him?* I watched as he tried to pull at the feathers that were now hugging him in an unnatural embrace.

A door swung open unexpectedly and flooded the room with bright and unnerving light. A woman appeared at the entrance and her eyes searched the room, paying close attention to us and the cages we were in.

"Thanks, Omar, for shouting up a storm." I said and gave him a vengeful look.

"I'm glad to see you are all up and well. We're lucky that the two of you survived." The unknown woman smiled at us.

"Why are we here? Who are you? What is going to happen to me?" Omar began to panic.

The stranger ignored him for a moment with a comical smile and then glanced over at Anon and me. "He sure does ask a lot of questions, doesn't he? I don't blame you, I did too when I first came here. My name is Mae. People always have many questions when they first enter into their calling." Her thin strawberry blonde hair swept over her back gracefully as she walked over to Anon's cylinder. I was able to sense that she was morphed too. *Are her clothes disguising an ability?* "What's your name again?"

"Anon."

"Is that short for 'anonymous'? Does that mean you don't have a name?" She grinned.

He chuckled. "I've heard that one before already. My name seems to have multiple meanings, two of them include: "Gift of God' or 'unknown person.'"

Omar rolled his eyes, "So, by definition, you're basically a pretentious nobody."

"Good one Omar. Glad to see you have some humor underneath all your panic." Anon looked at the woman in front of him. "Are you here to get us out?"

"That's actually going to be your job. We need to see if your morphing worked so we have to do a test run. Place any hand out in front of you and breathe in deeply. Don't stop breathing inwards... even if you feel lightheaded."

Anon followed her instructions and did as he was told and the veins in his arms began to glow bright. For some reason he looked as if he was about to cry. I had never seen him that scared before, not since the night he tried to swim out over to the light in the glowing sea. Up until now I had already assumed that Anon was insecure and trying to mask his self-esteem issues with poor jokes and rash actions, but before my own eyes I was seeing another layer of security being ripped away from under him. It was enjoyable to watch. I liked seeing Anon get tested. For some reason I felt as though he deserved anything coming to him.

"Exhale sharply." she stated, and a bolt of lightning began cutting through the glass in front of him. "Now carve a path out from it."

Omar and I watched in shock as Anon was able to accomplish this. The sound of the lightning was extremely loud and the entire room changed in color as he used it. He kept his eyes mostly closed as he moved his arm around, clearly scared that he would hurt himself or one of us by accident. Thankfully we were spread out enough that the rays didn't bring harm.

It looked like the last scrap of confidence within Anon had vanished away. "Am I even considered human anymore?" he asked Mae.

"Who ever said you were human in the first place?" She questioned back at him with a wink and unlocked mine and Omar's glass doors. "Our faction, the Over Grounds, will have to meet at the main base with the other two for the opening ceremony. The Land Dwellers are the group who reside in the jungle. The Oceanic Guardians are assigned to stay in the ocean with the exception of combat. The fighting doesn't start until after the ceremony though."

"I feel different. What has changed within me?" I asked.

Mae looked at me with what seemed to be tired eyes and took my hand in hers. "On your own time, test out your ability. I can see that it's within you and you survived being morphed so that's a good sign. I would assist you in your discovery too, but I have somewhere else to be right now."

I didn't respond to her but instead yanked my arm away. *Don't trust anyone.*

She accepted my silence and turned to exit the room, leaving us trapped with our own concerns and frustration. "You all will be assigned rooms and given the items you'll need to take care of yourselves to survive while in your new temporary home."

"Wait, I have a question!" Omar said while walking towards her.

"I'm sure each of you have a lot and most of them will be answered at the ceremony tomorrow." She didn't bother to turn around for him. *I wouldn't either.*

"Why did I not get morphed too?" Omar touched along his arms and face while looking at Anon and me with a confused expression.

"You just simply weren't chosen." Mae stated as she walked away.

"I'm going to excuse myself." I let my two acquaintances know. I needed fresh air away from all of the heightened stress that the two men were exuding.

"Make sure you stay safe." Omar replied as he went off to the room he was assigned to stay in. As we were parting ways, I heard him ask Anon, "How am I going to survive what's coming next?"

Three Months Before

"I can't believe you would put all of this together for me." Andrea said as they walked out onto Zayika's back patio. It was raining outside as they walked on wet grass towards a grey gazebo covered in plants growing along each side of it.

"It's your birthday Andrea, it's the least I could do. There's no way I would pass up on celebrating you turning twenty-two. Now we're the same age!" Zayika smiled as she turned on the fairy lights that had been placed underneath the cracking ceiling.

"I swear you get excited over everything." her friend responded as she took a seat next to the snack table. "Where is everyone else?"

"They will be here soon. Technically we both are early right now. I didn't think our hair appointment would be as quick as it was."

"Yeah the hairdresser was really talented. I think she did a great job on your hair, the white and purple really suits you."

"Thanks. I was a bit nervous that it would get messed up, but I prefer this over the brunette color."

"What time did you tell everyone to arrive?"

Zayika laughed as she finished setting up the drinks, "Don't worry. They should show up at any moment. Relax. I'll grab my speakers to put on some music for us."

Andrea waited in her seat as the sun fell lower in the sky. The lights became more vibrant against the wood they were strung across. The previously steady rainfall began to grow harsher as the wind picked up, blowing it around the yard and getting her hair and outfit wet. A half hour had passed by of waiting and she was beginning to get anxious.

"Zayika?" Andrea called out as she left the gazebo and headed back to the house.

Zayika sprinted out of her backyard doors with a flustered face and no speakers in her hands. "I'm sorry. My mom started talking to me and we lost track of time."

"It's okay, I guess. It's starting to get stormy out here, should we bring everything in?"

"No. Just leave it where it is." Zayika stepped out from under the doorframe and went back into the rain.

"You're getting all wet now too. I think everything out here will be ruined." Andrea started trailing behind her with her cold arms swaying limply by her sides. "Let's bring it inside."

Zayika spun around on the bottoms of her feet and her expression tightened angrily. "This is my house, not yours. This party was my idea, not yours. I will decide what happens tonight." Both women looked into each other's eyes momentarily as raindrops fell over their faces.

"What's wrong? Why are you mad?" Andrea's expression turned from confused to fearful.

"Because I don't like anyone telling me what to do."

"I'm sorry. I was just trying to make a s-suggestion." Zayika's friend stuttered.

"Where is everyone else? They should be here by now! I swear if they're ditching this party they don't know what will be coming after them." Zayika turned back around and sat on the slippery gazebo steps with her phone in hand.

"Is that supposed to be a threat?" Andrea kept her distance.

"Well actions should have consequences. My parents taught me that negligence needs to be reprimanded, especially against those who are being mindfully inconsiderate."

Present

I looked at the planet that we were on, in awe of its beauty, but also in confusion as to why we were taken there. The environment was eerie, to say the least and I sort of loved everything about it. *Is this planet a part of a greater purpose or a nightmare that has come to life?* Looking off in the distance, I could almost see three divisions of the planet as a whole laid out before me. I noticed that Gebu, Anon, a man named Nero, and another male stranger from our group had wings. I wished my ability was to fly. I wasn't sure what being morphed did to me since I hadn't tested my power yet. As I was thinking about the men being the only ones given the wings, not us women, I saw Anon behind me at an edge of the cliff. I realized quickly that he was outside too in order to practice flying. *It's a good thing he's practicing, at least.* Watching him wasn't as entertaining as I thought it would be since he ended up learning to maneuver his wings really fast. I watched him soar around a bit in the sky. *Must feel good.* He seemed to enjoy throwing himself into danger, being reckless, and acting like a daredevil so I wasn't surprised with how suddenly he became accustomed to jumping off of ledges.

I looked at my skin with some displeasure, *what is it I can even do?* I became distracted by Anon choosing to go down by the ocean's shore and Amira who started to come out of the water. *What in the world?* The two of them started conversing. I wasn't surprised that she was still alive and that she had a burnt orange tail behind her–I'll admit she looked sort of intriguing. *How many mermaids are there in the ocean?* I was bothered that Anon and her were talking because I knew that all of us were separated from one another for a reason. I couldn't help but watch them and imagine what they were saying... or plotting. The discussion that the two were having was extremely short lived, though, as Omar came outside and began calling out for Anon. I couldn't bring myself to care about their business. I looked at Anon rush away and back up to where we were, leaving Amira at the water.

I started to drift away with my thoughts. I took in a deep breath to use my ability, but nothing happened. *How did Anon cut the glass like he did?* I even attempted to tense up every muscle that I had and still nothing happened. I closed my eyes and focused on my body and found myself stuck with no progress. I was going to give up and return inside when I saw a small group of people on the sand from the corner of my eye. They were holding spears and yelling towards the ocean. I walked closer to the edge of the platform I was on to get a better look. It seemed to be three individuals who came from the jungle area due to their attire and choices of words.

"Get out of the water and let's get this over with!" One of them yelled. "Us Land Dwellers will survive this challenge!"

The three others were on the shore and four individuals rose slightly out of the ocean water, I noticed that Amira was one of them. I could feel the tension in the air as they all stared threateningly at one another. *Why are people attacking each other here?*

Amira spoke first amongst her group. "Go away. Why act rash towards us Oceanic Guardians? Let's hear what is said at the opening ceremony before we take actions against one another."

"We're not leaving! There's no sense in waiting until the opening ceremony, we need you gone!" they replied while raising spears into the air along with a few hand-crafted weapons.

One of the women on Amira's side was suddenly struck in her chest by one of their weapons, resulting in the Land Dwellers celebrating by charging towards their rivaling faction. I wanted to involve myself in this fight so I could try to figure out what I was capable of. I made my way over to the platform to get down to the ground but rushed too quickly. As I stepped downwards from a rock, I cleanly sliced off a piece of my skin right above my heel. I winced out loud as I saw blood falling. I regretted trying to join the others, and my skin started to beam with a faint yellow light. My hands shone the most vividly and I placed one of them on the wound I had just received. *There's no way... I can heal.* My skin went back to normal as all of the stinging subsided. *Could I also inflict damage with this ability?* My intuition told me I was capable of more.

I watched on as both groups decided to attack one another. A man from the ocean tried to shoot seaweed from his hands to choke a Dweller member but missed.

"This is your last warning." Amira cautioned them, "Go away."

They ignored her and kept running forwards. Amira's group was not doing well as they were taken by surprise. Two more members of her faction were killed by arrows. She started to direct a large wave at the three of the land fighters in anger as she became their final target.

A man threw the spear near Amira's face and narrowly missed as it plunged deep in the water next to her. "You need to be eliminated!"

"Hippo... attack." Amira said calmly.

A large rumble stemming from the ocean began to shake the ground underneath all of us. I watched in horror as the waters started to light up brightly. Amira went back under as the largest living creature I had ever seen started to make its presence known. A beaming orb rose upwards, hanging from the end of a long wire-like appendage. The orb was shocking in size until I saw what it was attached to. It shoved heaping amounts of waves out of the way and pushed the sand back too. Jagged teeth arose from the darkness and the rushing sound of falling water created a small earthquake. The teeth that the creature had were larger than any tree on this planet.

"There's no way." I said under my breath. *Is that an... anglerfish?*

I ended up being right and had no idea how what I was watching was possible. The three men started screaming for their lives and tried to run in the opposite direction, attempting to retreat back into hiding.

"It's too late for you all." Amira said in a low and menacing voice while springing out from the waves. The fish's jaws opened wide as it lunged itself forwards and forcefully bit downwards, taking a part of the shore into its mouth along with the men, killing them. I watched on blissfully, enjoying the intensity of the events taking place. There was the sound of an ear-splitting snap that rang out. The fish had cracked one of its gigantic teeth while aggressively biting.

Amira was horrified as she yelled, "Hippo!"

What kind of name is 'Hippo'?

The fish let out a wail of pain as it began to go back completely into the water.

My eyes felt as though they were darting around everywhere, my heart was racing faster than it ever had before. "What just happened?" I asked myself out loud.

"You did it, Hippo, good girl. You saved my life." Amira touched the side of the giant anglerfish and went underneath the heavy waters with her.

That's her fighting companion? Lucky.

CHAPTER SEVEN: SURVIVAL OF THE MENTALLY FITTEST

Omar

Present

I felt odd as a new day started. We were told by Mae that we were going to have to attend a ceremony, so I was ready to finally receive some answers. I got ready and met with Anon and Zayika before leaving. I watched as Anon touched his wings; he seemed wary of them, but also mesmerized in a way. I started to wonder what it would've been like to have a power given to me. I thought about Mae telling me that I wasn't 'chosen.' *What did that mean?* It hurt to hear, but I tried to not question my self-worth or importance. I knew we were in danger and without an ability, I felt that I was the weakest and most vulnerable version of myself. I leaned into the corner of a wall, almost drowning in my own thoughts. I watched on as Anon and Zayika began comparing their morphed differences between one another. *Even on a different planet, I'm still an outsider...*

"Your freckles do look really cool, though." he told her as tiny stars glistened under the artificial light we were under.

"I wonder what makeup concepts could be made from this?" she asked as her new form seemed to have oddly started growing on her.

"Imagine going to a cosplay convention and shocking everyone. Pretending like this is makeup and then shooting a literal lightning bolt out of my arms." Anon couldn't stop staring at his new body. "I need to keep practicing flying. It's a good thing I'm not scared of heights like Omar."

Thanks Anon.

"Guess what." Zayika looked mischievous, as she often did.

"What is it?" Anon fluttered his wings a bit–trying to discover how well he could control moving them around.

"I got to try out my ability earlier. It turns out that I can heal myself. This means that I can probably heal others too."

"No way! That's awesome! That will definitely come in handy and would have been useful back at the bunker when Omar cut his hand." Anon told her.

Why bring that up?

"It's fine. It was a miniscule scratch." I stated. I didn't want others to simply see me as weak.

"Apparently I can cut glass so I must be able to really hurt someone with this lightning." Anon redirected the topic of discussion.

"I'm sure you can." Zayika looked slightly envious. "I hope I can hurt others too."

Anon and I gave her odd looks amongst some awkward silence.

"I-I worded that wrong. I meant my ability might have two uses: defense and healing. At least I hope it does." She tried to cover up what seemed to be hidden motives.

"Well good for you guys." I grunted. *Maybe I am the envious one?* I felt completely out of luck. Not only had I been taken to a dangerous and puzzling planet so far away from home, but I was stuck with no powers and with two others who seemed to not care about me that much. I started to ponder the personalities of both Anon and Zayika and understand who they were and where they came from. *Try to see the best in everyone. Maybe these two will help protect me. Don't be jealous.*

"Do you think that we will stay this way forever?" Zayika began to place her silver and purple hair into a messy bun.

"Don't know, that's a good question, one I'd rather not get too worried about in the moment. Hopefully this ceremony that we're about to go to will address these concerns like Mae stated." I was trying hard to stay calm.

I went over to a window nearby and was overwhelmed at what I saw. We were so high up into the sky and the clouds didn't look normal to me-they were lumpy and made it seem as though the ocean waves were above us. I wanted the tools to paint and document what I was seeing. The planet didn't seem inviting, just like the people who inhabited it. I looked down and could see the cliffs drop off into oblivion right next to our floating terrain. I wanted to throw up and gripped the windowsill with sweaty fingertips. Every stressor in my mind started to invade my emotions at once. *Am I useless? Am I never going to be someone who is chosen for anything?* I felt purposeless like an inanimate object trapped in a snow globe viewing a giant's hand about to shake and turn everything upside down.

"I saw Amira yesterday." Zayika pulled me out of my thoughts as she spoke to us, but her words seemed targeted at Anon.

"How was she doing?" Anon's interest became evident.

I kept staring outside while the two were talking to each other. I could hardly focus on anything Zayika was saying. Impending doom started to encompass my thoughts. *What's out there? What if I can't fight back?*

"Did you know she has a massive creature to command around?"

"Um... yeah. Hippo? She's pretty cool, huh?" Anon sounded thrilled. "I mean she's a colossal anglerfish! I didn't even realize they could get that big. I wonder what other mutated creatures there must be on this planet."

"Enough about the fish. What is it that you two do together? I noticed you spending some time with her by the ocean." Zayika stated suspiciously as I continued to listen on.

"We just talk. She's my friend. You know, we all should be friends with her. She was a great addition to our group when we met on the hills."

"What does it feel like?" I asked, interrupting their conversation. "Your powers? I'm really curious."

"I feel like I can do anything." Anon looked at me. "I don't know how to describe it. I feel important."

A small stab of curiosity taunted me. "I wonder why I wasn't chosen. Maybe there are others from the different factions that weren't chosen too?"

"Or maybe you're simply the standard boy next door. This could mean they will just send you home!" Anon hit me over the head lightly, causing a small spark to whirr in my ears.

"Ow! Be careful with your hands!" I winced and rubbed my head.

"Sorry about that." He turned away from me. "Omar, look, maybe you will get powers later. Or honestly maybe you're just not supposed to be here."

Zayika walked closer to me. "Did you have an odd dream before you were taken to this planet like Anon and Saige did?"

One Year Before

"I hope that you both sleep well too." Omar his parents before going upstairs to his room. He checked his phone and saw no messages. After turning on his lights, he settled into his bed. Time-lapses of various artists painting original pieces were his choice of videos to watch for relaxation before sleep. He tiredly watched on as a bouquet of white roses was being crafted carefully by each brushstroke of one of his favorite creators online. A soft buzz and glow from his phone redirected his attention as he swiped the screen to answer it.

"Hey, I've been waiting for your call." He sat up against his pillows. "Are you as nervous for tomorrow's final as I am?"

His friend, Zyair, spoke quickly back to him. "I'm terribly nervous. Don't mind the background noise. I'm baking right now."

"Why are you baking? It's almost one in the morning." Omar laughed as he rolled onto his stomach, adjusting his neck for support.

"You know my sleep schedule is screwed. Plus this final has been weighing heavily on my shoulders. I haven't done too well on our smaller assignments, as you know, so there's a lot of pressure riding on this grade. Not to mention that our professor is as biased as they come."

"He has favorites for sure."

"I swear some of our classmates don't even try to incorporate the techniques that we learn, and they get radiant grades. What is that about?"

"I don't know. Personally I feel like they try too hard to get his attention and they cut corners." Omar picked at the leftover yellow paint that was underneath his nails. "Zyair I don't know how to stand out."

"It will come naturally by accepting who you are as a person. Don't worry about others in class, most of them aren't showing their real personalities anyways." There was a brief silence. "By the way, I've actually been meaning to ask you what topic you chose for your final piece?"

"Interpersonal conflict."

"What does the concept of it look like so far? We have another week before it's due, but I know you already have an image in your head for it."

"I chose to paint a leaky boat lost on a raging sea."

"Interesting. Is that supposed to be a representation of yourself in some way?" A timer rang out. "Oh! Wait hold on, I forgot something in the oven."

Omar waited for a few moments for Zyair to get back on the phone. He started to question what his painting represented. He didn't know where it came from and found himself asking the same question in his mind as Zyair.

"I'm going to get some rest, okay? Can we talk tomorrow?" Omar got up to turn his room lights off and get ready for bed.

"Yeah dude that's cool. I'll text you. Sleep well."

The two exchanged goodnights with one another and Omar fell into his blankets a little while later.

Present

I crossed my arms together. "No, I didn't have a dream."

"Oh okay, don't read too far into it, Anon and I aren't." Zayika gave him a peculiar look and then glanced back at me.

"Speak for yourself, I'm most certainly reading into my dream." Anon said. "There's got to be a reason why I had it presented to me. There's no way those dreams weren't preparing us for something astronomical. What if we're meant to save mankind?"

Zayika rolled her eyes and whispered something in his ear. He rolled his brown eyes back and faced her, whispering indistinctly.

"I'm right here." I told them as I dragged my foot against the room's glossy tiles.

"Sorry Omar." Zayika nudged Anon.

"Yeah, sorry if you feel left out. I doubt we're here to save the human race or do anything of epic sorts."

You don't have to rub it in...

The door to our room swung in rapidly. Mae was fuming as she looked at us three. "What are you all doing here still talking? You're late! Get on the platform now, this ceremony is not something to be taken lightly!"

My heart rate spiked as I followed Anon and Zayika, who were guided by Mae's steps. We walked through multiple empty corridors and then down a few flights of stairs leading us outside. We were taken down from the sky similar to the way we had come up from on the moving platform. I couldn't hold any of my thoughts together as we headed towards the event. Zayika put her arms stiffly around Anon and me as we were lowered to the planet's surface. This brought a ray of comfort over me for a brief moment as I felt that I wasn't alone in this struggle. I only had a limited amount of information. I knew that Anon and Zayika both were given abilities that I wasn't, and what they were given were drastically different from one another. I also knew that all three of us now belonged to the same faction named the Over Grounds in reference to our sky-bound location.

Unfortunately, that was the extent of it; I didn't know what planet we were on or what the ceremony would be for. I only could sense that fighting was bound to take place soon and that I had never fought before. As we arrived at our destination, there were three trumpets that rang out seeming to signal that we, the final faction, had arrived. We were assigned a certain section in a grassy field across from a large cliff that had what looked to be a handmade podium placed on the edge of it. We were also told to stand and await instructions patiently and to not interact with the other two factions. After what felt like an hour of waiting, three representatives from each faction made their way up to speak at all of us below. I spotted Amira, Saige, and Zekiel as they made brief eye contact with Anon, Zayika, and me. Two women and one man stood before us. They were dressed nicely and stood tall in preparation for their speech. One woman was a representative from the faction that Amira belonged to.

"Hello everyone. I am from the Oceanic Guardians faction." She forced a smile. "This will be the only instance of us all meeting together in this way. I have been tasked with the responsibility of clearing up the purpose of this situation for all of you before you begin the fight. Not only this speech, but the battle itself, will go by quickly. In fact, I'm sure the preparation and anticipation feel as though they will last a lifetime in comparison to what lies ahead. I encourage you all to appreciate this stage as much as you can. By now you all have been morphed. We promise to make this presentation brief for the sake of those who need to return to the water in a timely manner."

She was wrong... not all of us had been changed... am I really the only one who hasn't been? It seemed to turn from overcast to overwhelmingly sunny in just moments. Many of us put our arms up in order to shield the light from our eyes. I wanted to put my arm up high and ask why I wasn't morphed too, but I discovered I didn't have the courage.

"The three factions here consist of the Oceanic Guardians, Over Grounds, and the Land Dwellers. Each faction contains ten members taken from diverse areas from Earth and from varying social classes, backgrounds, and skills. You all were chosen as members in this battle for a reason. The planet we are on does not have a name to our current knowledge though it would be fitting to refer to it as some type of a mental playground. All of you will be tested in some way and many will lose your lives at the hands of a different faction than your own."

The air grew thicker as each word was spoken. The collective silence was as heavy as the fate that awaited us.

She continued, "I will try to explain this as well as I can. Only one faction will make it out alive, whether that be a group of people from one, or just a single individual. You will be competing to be the last standing. Those who naturally survive from the same group will be able to go back to Earth and return to the home from which they were taken. There is a catch, however, that the survivor or multiple survivors will get to change one part of their life forever in their journey back. Whether that be receiving fame and fortune, wishing for immortality, bringing a loved one back from the dead, being given a second chance, or even undoing a past mistake would be possible because the opportunities for the final wish will be endless. The point in this all is to value the prize that is life and to sharpen everyone's understanding of what it is they want for their destiny. Who has questions?"

Multiple hands flew into the air as the stakes were raised high and the chance of survival for many of us became obsolete. She called on Zekiel first.

"What is your question, Zekiel from the Land Dweller faction?

He inched forward. "What would happen if someone was to commit suicide here? Would they return to Earth?"

She paused before responding to him, "Do you have a death wish? Of course they wouldn't. I don't understand what type of question that is."

"No, I was just wondering wh–" He retreated. "Forget I asked anything." Zekiel's face flushed red.

Saige looked at him with concern in her eyes and spoke up over the brewing silence. "I want to clarify that two people from one faction can both make it back home, right?" She took Zekiel's hand in hers. "Would only one get to pick a wish or would both people have that chance?"

"Both individuals would get a wish of their own, Saige. If five people from the Land Dweller faction made it out alive, they would get to all make one major decision for the life they're returning to. That would result in five wishes total being granted."

Amira waved her hand slightly to draw attention to be called on. "Why were we specifically picked? Will there be others that are chosen after us?"

"Yes, well that's what we were told. A new batch of people will be selected for each faction after this battle is over. I cannot answer your first question, that is left open to your own interpretation."

A man from my faction pushed through a few of us to become the center of attention. "My name is Nero, you guys will want to remember that. I'm sort of the main character around here." Echoes of 'shut up Nero' could be heard from those around who already knew him. "I'm willing to do whatever it takes to survive. Literally."

The presenter was pleased by his comment. "That's good to hear. Those given abilities should use them wisely, whether it be crafting weapons or using the force of nature's elements against others. Be actively mindful of your weaknesses and your strengths. Take time to cool down if you need to, but don't let your guard down or else... you may die."

"It feels like we're in a video game." I heard Nero state excitedly.

"Make sure you don't take an arrow to the knee." Anon whispered back as a joke.

Apparently each group was supposed to have ten individuals within them. I noticed that Nero was missing one of his wings, seeing the wound where his other wing used to be made me feel sick. I took a headcount of the other groups and discovered that they didn't have a complete ten like we did. *The killings have already started...*

"We three representatives will remain alive until there is one faction standing. As we can see, some of you have already started the killing due to the lack of numbers. More power to you. We will be on standby near the starting hills for those who have questions. From now until tomorrow you can reside at your faction headquarters and, well, start the fighting when you see fit. Please exit without violence at this time. Once nightfall is upon us, you can resume the killing."

CHAPTER EIGHT: FREE OF CHARGE

Omar

Present

It was the day after the ceremony and Anon and I were in hiding. I felt bad about all of the bickering that had taken place between us up until then. With the possibility of dying at any moment, I wanted to make amends with him just in case something happened to either of our lives. Even though I felt that Anon could be rash in regard to his decision making, I did like certain parts of his personality. *The two of us could make good friends.* When I would think about the first few hours I had on the hills, I would shudder. I truly believed I was losing my mind and was utterly and tragically alone. Anon finding and letting me join him and the rest was a small piece of acceptance and inclusion that I had been longing for. Seeing his face in the midst of so much anxiety raining down on me helped put my mind at ease. When I would look at him, I'd remember when we first met. *It's okay to agree to disagree with others. Having differences is healthy. Be a friend to him.* Even if his jokes weren't always funny, it was nice that he tried to ease the tension and make tough situations easier to get through. He reminded me of my friend Zyair... who I wasn't sure I'd ever get to see again.

"Since we're a part of the same faction, I think we should start getting along more." I said to Anon as we waited outside of the Land Dweller's retreating space.

"I wonder how long Zekiel is going to take." He avoided acknowledging my statement, "I don't want to get noticed by anyone from this faction."

"Are you not listening to me?"

"I am. I mean, yeah, I guess we could try to work on developing a friendship."

"What is it about me that you have a problem with?"

Anon stopped to think for a moment at my words. "Honestly? I don't think you make a very good team member sometimes. You think based on your emotions a lot and I feel that makes you... weak. On top of that you don't have any abilities to show for it so it's hard to take direction from you seriously."

"You don't think that I give good advice?"

"I don't know, Omar. I don't know how to word it to you. I'm sorry if I sound harsh. Maybe we just have differences. I don't think you're a bad person though."

I tried to pay attention to the good in what he said. "That does mean a lot to me Anon. Thank you for saying that. For the record, I don't think you're a bad person either."

He looked off into different directions to avoid eye contact. *Does he not believe me?*

"He should be coming out any minute." Anon said.

"Wait–what is it we are doing here? Was there something I missed during the ceremony? You've forced me to come with you here and barely talked on the way so what's going on?"

"Nero shared something with me. He told me that he was attacked by Zekiel and Saige's group. That's how he lost a wing. He also said that they threatened to come after us next. I don't think that sounds like them, but I wanted to come here and see the truth for myself. I doubt they're really plotting anything."

I felt like my jaw hit the floor. "Why did you make me come here with you?" My anxiety started to spike.

"Shh! Don't raise your voice. They are right over there now."

The front gates amongst the vines opened, drawing both of our attention to Zekiel, who was walking out of the building. There were a few members of his faction beside him and Saige wasn't anywhere to be seen.

"Looks like they're having an important conversation. Let's see what we can hear." Anon stealthily made his way near them, making sure to stay out of view.

I reluctantly followed after deciding it wasn't worth a disagreement to not follow his plan. *Pick your battles wisely... pick them with more wisdom than you have in the past.*

"We don't know who you are, sir." We saw Zekiel say as he took brave steps towards a stranger who approached them. "Why should we even trust what you have to say?"

"My name is Nathaniel. I'm a Land Dweller." A man in ragged clothes said. "I'm fifty-four years old and have lived on this planet for over twenty so I think I might be able to offer you some advice. I even know of a valuable stone on this planet that you probably haven't even seen before."

"That doesn't make any sense. We previously had our complete ten, but unfortunately are at six casualties now." one of the Land Dwellers in the group replied. "How could you be one of us? We have never seen you before."

"I'm from a previous battle that took place many years ago. The representatives neglected to inform you of the true past and current history of this planet. I listened in on that pathetic excuse of a presentation." Dirt covered his entire body. "I survived through hiding. There is a bunker that I've inhabited, and to my luck, it hasn't been taken away from me so far."

Anon peered over his shoulder at me. We both exchanged glances. This man was the same one we ran into and stole from when we first arrived.

"You're the man who was sleeping?" Zekiel stopped walking and finally gave Nathaniel his full attention.

"I'm glad you remember me. You and the others that you were with didn't know I was there until a woman found my mattress."

"Yes, her name is Amira. I also remember that you threatened us."

"Don't judge actions when they're in self-defense. You were raiding my property. I had a right to scare you all away."

"I'm glad we've established this. Although, what is it that you're really wanting to talk to me about? Because I have a feeling that it's not about the items we took."

"Let's talk privately." Nathaniel said to Zekiel as he pulled him aside. "You need to understand the unique situation that you are in. The current faction members don't know this because they didn't exist in the last batch like I did." Nathaniel pointed lazily to the other men who were previously involved in the conversation.

"They don't know about what?"

"The group you arrived with in the hills has three Wish Carriers within it."

"What are you talking about?" Zekiel asked.

"The ceremony didn't tell you everything. You weren't told about the information from the stone. They want you all to think that you walk on equal grounds, that rules are the same no matter what group we come from, but that's not the case. Out of the six of you who intruded into my bunker, there are three Wish Carriers."

"What is a 'Wish Carrier' and how would you know that?" Zekiel asked him. "We ran away out of the bunker and didn't even talk to you."

"You didn't have to talk to me. I overheard the conversation that was taking place between one of the men and women about having dreams. On the planet's stone, it is engraved that Wish Carriers are the real key out of this game and are given this responsibility through a dream."

"Anon and Saige were the ones sharing their dream stories with one another." Zekiel's expression grew more worrisome.

I looked at Anon, who sat terrified at the conversation we were eavesdropping in on. He stared at Nathaniel and Zekiel intently, hoping to hear more information about his apparent calling.

"Are either of them a Land Dweller?" Nathaniel kicked a thick layer of mud off of his boots as he carried on the exchange.

"Yes, Saige is one." Zekiel turned to look at her in the faction's courtyard. "What does that mean?"

"Wish Carriers are pivotal in going home. They are the secret that the faction representatives don't want to share. Those who are given this title are the holders of one wish. If they survive... they get a wish and get to go home. But if they are murdered, well, whoever killed them gets their wish."

"Why wouldn't they tell us this at the ceremony?"

"Because they don't want you to know the truth. Those without a wish, if they somehow survive, would be stuck here until the next Wish Carriers are brought along and who knows how long that could be. Saige needs to be protected. You need to keep her wish in your hands."

"So that means Anon is a Wish Carrier too then?"

"The other one with the dream? Yes. The importance that they hold can hardly be described in words. They are the true key in getting back to Earth."

"How is their wish obtained?"

"Murder, as I just shared."

Anon stood up slowly while remaining out of their view. He paced back and forth behind the wall we were hiding behind and started gnawing at his own lip again. "Cut that out before you hurt yourself like last time, man." I whispered to him.

"I won't let Saige die. Thank you for sharing this information with me, Nathaniel." Zekiel reached to shake his hand politely.

"There's something else I need to tell you about the other man in your group." Nathaniel physically pulled Zekiel away from the other men to continue their conversation privately. Thankfully they walked closer to our direction instead of away from it. "What's his name?"

"Omar, why?"

I felt my stomach drop as I heard my name mentioned. I listened worriedly to what was said next.

"He's one hundred percent human. He has no morphed abilities and had no prior dream to his arrival which means he has no calling. Mae from the Over

Grounds faction, where he was placed, was speaking to others outside about how she found out he's not morphed after the ceremony was over."

"What?"

"This means he's a freebee. He's a walking wish waiting to get taken. I don't think he will live long, especially if this information gets out to the other factions, which I would advise you to make sure that won't happen. Pure humans, also known as 'commoners,' don't appear here often. In fact, I have only read about them on some of the planet's stone before a part of it was catastrophically swept away out to sea in a storm. He will hardly be able to defend himself. If I were you, I would protect Saige and kill Omar. It's your only chance at you both getting a wish and sent home. Almost everyone will die, Zekiel.

The faction representatives want you all to believe that this is a game about the last ones standing but it's not. This game is about stealing from others, ripping away their light so that you can shine in whatever your wish may be, even if it is darkness. You should keep carrying on. You've let me talk enough. I wanted you to hear this from me first. Tomorrow I plan on directly sharing this information about Anon and Omar with the rest of the Land Dwellers as I'm prepared to answer whatever questions they throw at me. You should sleep on this information since it's turning into nightfall."

Six Months Before

The professor stood at the front of the classroom with a black felt-tip marker in hand. "Who's ready to present their piece first? Please state your name, age, painting's name, and theme of choice before quoting the writing you've paired along with it."

The classroom was silent as all of the seniors nervously waited for anyone but themselves to do the first presentation. Omar saw this as his chance to shine and raised his hand to catch his professor's attention. The teacher nodded for him to exit his desk and began sharing with his classmates the work he had put together once he reached the front of the room.

"Hello everyone. My name is Omar and I'm twenty-two years old. The name of my painting is *The Depth of the Ocean* and its theme is the study of interpersonal conflict." He placed his painting on the small metal ledge of the whiteboard to show the class. A fragile leaking boat caught within a plummeting wave was the central focus of the piece he had created. Dark clouds were placed over the boat as rain fell steadily underneath them. The ocean waves were painted with great attention to detail, each brushstroke telling a small story of their own in an unspoken way.

"You did a good job on your technique, Omar." The professor said at the corner of the room. "You can now read the script that you crafted to accompany it."

Omar cleared his throat and looked down at his shoes. "If you act out these words you can use this poem for meditation." After letting out a deep breath he grabbed the crumpled paper from his pocket that he printed his words on earlier that day. He nervously started reading out loud, "Close your eyes. Find the depth within yourself. Breathe in deeply. Can't you hear it? The sound of the ocean rolling away from the sandy shore? Breathe out deeply. Can't you hear it? The sound of the cold air sweeping over the salty waves that crash over heavy rocks? You only see darkness, just like the night sky with no stars in sight. The ocean breathes along with you."

Present

"What is going on? I don't want to die." My thoughts were colliding against one another distractingly as I headed back to our faction with Anon. "I can't believe I was called a 'freebee', do you understand how insulting that is?"

The platform came to a halt as we walked over to the opening iron gates. It was nice of him to take the longer way up with me because I couldn't fly. We passed several angel statues as the front door came into view with bushes lined neatly beside us.

"Sorry about that, man. You need to learn to accept that you don't have abilities." Anon responded. "I guess we just have to keep an eye out and be careful what we do. We should also keep that conversation between the two of us. The last thing we need is a chaotic war breaking out over who gets to claim one of our lives first."

"I don't think Nathaniel should be trusted. What if he's lying?" I said.

"Nathaniel?" Gebu appeared from behind one of the bushes. "I met him."

Anon and I leapt into the air, slightly surprised by the sudden interaction as we were already on our guard for a potential attack.

"Oh, it's just you again." Anon sighed with relief and a hint of annoyance.

"Yes it's me Anon, you can lower your lightning lasers." Gebu's bright green eyes curiously darted back and forth between the two of us. "Nathaniel is a pretty weird guy, no?"

Anon raised both of his eyebrows. "You of all people are calling him 'weird'? That's rich."

I lightly shoved Anon in response to his Gebu, "Be nice." I whispered in cringeworthy silence.

"Don't worry Omar, I get that a lot, but thanks for sticking up for me." Gebu climbed out of the branches and leaves to pull a small snack out of his pocket to eat. "I ran into Nathaniel when I was trying to familiarize myself with this planet after appearing here. I used exploration as an opportunity to practice flying. I'm actually the first male in our faction to have wings."

"Is that why they're so much smaller than the rest of ours?" Anon asked as his lips started to curl into a smile of mockery.

I nudged Anon again. "I think your wings look cool Gebu."

"Oh come on Omar, for being so obsessed with having morals you sure can tell a bold-faced lie." Anon laughed out loud.

"For some reason they seem to be the center of everyone's attention. I've been called a 'fairy' many times, especially by Nero, but I take it as a compliment that he can't stop commenting on them. I stand out from the rest." Gebu looked at his wings proudly. "They get me where I need to go so who cares what anyone else thinks?"

"So what did Nathaniel say to you?" Anon asked nervously.

"Very concerning information actually." Gebu put a finger up to us as he took another bite of food.

As we waited for him to continue, Anon and I exchanged worried looks, quietly communicating our concerns for what we would hear next.

"Did you talk to him at his bunker?" I asked to try to hurry the conversation along.

Gebu swallowed some of his snack and gave a shocked expression. "That man was in a bunker? That's epic."

"Yeah, you'd think his alternate name is Desmond with his power here being time traveling." Anon was the only one who laughed, I was unable to find anything funny in that moment.

"I ran into him when he was in the jungle out looking for food and water." Gebu responded.

"What did he tell you?" I asked impatiently.

"That the two of us are out of luck." Gebu locked eyes with Anon. "Our wings make us superior, but they also put us at a danger far beyond our worst nightmares. Nathaniel told me that if both of them are removed, we get punished by the planet and are forced into a never-ending loop of consuming darkness!"

I heard Anon swallow loudly. "What does that mean?"

"Not sure, but I definitely don't want to find out. Nathaniel offered to show me part of the planet's stone up close, but I turned down that tempting offer." Gebu said sarcastically. "I didn't need to know any more than that. But if either of you are wondering if the stone is real, I will swear to you that it is. I saw it with my own eyes from far away. All I know is to tell you, Anon, to make sure you protect your wings."

"I swear each minute we're on this planet everything makes less sense." Anon started to walk away from us slowly.

"I know what will lighten the mood! Let's all explore a bit together. I can give a quick tour of the different sights you will see here." Gebu's eagerness showed from his expression. "Maybe if we're lucky Nero will join us too."

"Nero's a flaming and uncontrollable narcissistic goon who we are better off without." Anon picked up his pace and began walking quickly ahead. "I can't stand that he's in our faction. He doesn't give a damn about any of us."

"Hey, just a minute ago you weren't so fond of me either, based off of your whispering to Omar." Gebu responded as we started to jog to catch up with him.

"Yes, but at least I would never willingly harm you like Nero would. Sometimes I jokingly make fun of my own people, but I only do so because they're my friends." Anon couldn't help but smile at the two of us as he looked backwards slightly.

"We're 'friends'?" I asked him.

"Yeah, Omar, I guess so." He kicked a few leaves underneath his feet. "We're a part of the coolest faction, right? We need to look out for each other."

"It felt like a long time waiting for you final six to arrive so the game here could start. I heard you showed up with a group of people but then got separated not long after? I spawned alone so I wouldn't know what that's like. Do you consider those placed into rivaling factions as your allies still?" Gebu already pulled a new snack from his pocket and offered us some.

"Yeah I still consider them my friends. I especially try to look out for Amira because I don't want her getting lonely. It's been a secret that we meet up." Anon looked at the ocean and started to eat from Gebu's share of food.

"So you do talk to her?" I met his walking speed at his right side, "She really doesn't attack you?"

"We keep our matters private Omar." Anon placed his hands into his pockets. "Why hurt each other if we don't have to?"

Gebu shrugged and surveyed Anon closely, "You sure she doesn't have a thing for you? Or that you have a thing for her?"

Anon's eyes widened as he started to laugh. "Man get out of here! You joke too much. My meetups with Amira are not... flirty like that."

"She doesn't sing you siren songs?" Gebu teased him.

"Nah dude we're just friends. She keeps to herself, even within her own faction, but I feel like deep down in her emotions she needs someone else to talk to. I like to be an outlet for her and listen to what she has to say." Anon looked over at me. "Omar, you don't talk to her? I mean right after arriving here she was the first friendly person we met."

I looked at the ground again. "I haven't spoken to her since you almost died at sea. I'm glad to hear that she's doing well though." Something about Amira honestly intimidated me, I couldn't find her easy to talk to like Anon did.

Gebu walked ahead of us and threw his arms up into the air. "Now it's time for the grand tour of the planet! The name is still unknown to everyone and is clearly divided into three main sections–not counting the hills and wheat field. Firstly, there is the superior chunk that resides high up in the air. As you know, our terrain is only accessible by flight or by using the rising platform that... is personally a little slow for my taste, but thankfully I have wings. Cooler temperatures reside higher up in the air accompanied by many gusts of wind. Our faction is without a doubt the best place to watch the sunset."

"This guy is a bit much..." Anon tried to whisper to me but I hushed him so we wouldn't talk behind Gebu's back.

"The second chunk is the jungle belonging to the Land Dwellers. Lots of humidity, fog and tangled vines there so it's not a solid place to go for a run. The third is the ocean and whatever is lurking within its depths, which is where the Oceanic Guardians reside. I've heard several stories that there are giant beasts that live and thrive under the water. I wouldn't know personally if they exist or not as I'm not much of a swimmer myself. Despite all of that I think it's the most peaceful location that exists here at the end of the day."

"Why don't we conclude this visit at the ocean then? It's been a while since I've had a beach day." I suggested.

"I'm okay with that. As long as we stay out of the view from hostile mermaids then I'll have a good time." Gebu responded. "Maybe we can visit with Amira and learn some of her inside jokes with Anon?"

"I'm right here." Anon joined in again. "As I said before, she is just my friend. For the record, she has been a good one to me."

The three of us walked towards the ocean as the bright hot day turned into a cooler evening. I was excited to return to the sand and waves. I loved the ocean and everything about it. The familiar smell of saltwater and sand crabs scurrying under my feet made me feel like I was back at home with my family. Living near the beach was one of the highlights I had while growing up. I wanted to tell Anon and Gebu stories from some of those times but didn't feel like they would care. The planet we were on was horrifying, but I was glad that it at least had a piece of life that made me feel at peace with my own self. I was eager to take my shoes off and feel the warm grains of sand again. After what felt like a few hours of traveling on dirt, we finally reached the point where sand was under the bottoms of our feet. Off in the distance we could see three individuals swimming, which I presumed were members of the Oceanic Guardian faction. We kept our distance from them at first while we visited with each other on the shore.

"Have you ever killed anyone Gebu?" Anon asked.

Who even starts a conversation like that? I gave Anon a look of shock for bringing up the topic that he did.

"No. My only power of flying isn't that useful in regard to self-defense and unfortunately I don't have the best hand-eye coordination. What about you both?" Gebu took a seat in the sand as Anon and I followed suit.

"Of course not." I chimed in since the answer to this question was easy. "Even thinking about inflicting physical harm to another person makes me sick. It's unfortunate that we've been brought onto a planet that normalizes pain and tries to justify taking the lives of others. Plus we haven't been here as long as you have, Gebu, and I most definitely haven't killed anyone before being taken here. I'm not a sadistic criminal."

"I haven't killed anyone either." Anon answered also. *Well geez... that's good.* "Although I'm ready to defend myself if the time comes. I don't want to be trapped in a place like this forever. Being here has helped me realize how valuable my old life was and the simple fact that I had my own freedom to enjoy parts of the world I seemed to take for granted."

"What would you consider those to be?" Gebu asked.

"Late night drives along backroads. Spending time with friends. Traveling. Participating in family traditions even through forced smiles. Spending time with this girl I met named Estrella, she was a great girlfriend to me, until she wasn't." Anon had taken off his shoes too after I did and shoved his feet down into the sand. "I could go on for too long about a list of things I miss from home. I just want to remain hopeful that I will get to go back, that we will get to go back, and return to those that miss us."

"Definitely." I agreed promptly. *At least Anon has some sense and wise words to share at times.*

"Omar, are you willing to do what it takes if the time comes to kill another person?" Anon asked me.

I felt my chest tighten as I heard the question being asked. While looking at Anon I could see five blurry shapes coming into a sharper view behind him. "Look! Something is happening!"

Gebu and Anon followed my gaze and also noticed the group that had formed as we talked with one another. There were four of our own faction in an argument with three Oceanic Guardian members that we saw earlier.

"This isn't good, you guys need to go do something!" Gebu started to panic.

"What do you mean by 'you guys'? You're a part of the same faction, let's all go help!" Anon jumped up as his arms started to glow. "We need to help them fight."

"I should let you know that I don't have extra powers in case you forgot already. I mean I can fly, so I'm not totally useless, sorry Omar…" Gebu sighed. "I'm only going to slow you guys down."

"Now isn't the time to hang back. We need to group together during these times." Anon led the way as I followed behind him with Gebu reluctantly dragging his feet behind me.

"Anon you are bringing along two people with you that really have no powers to offer; how are you this sure about doing this?" I asked him as we headed towards the fight.

"I feel like I need to help. Just like my dream that called me here, my mind is leading me to assist." he responded with growing confidence.

There were various abilities being used before us. I was in awe of the capabilities that everyone else except me had. I wondered what it was like for them to be able to harness and unleash the type of powers that they were able to now. *Why wasn't I given anything? Is there something I can't see in this circumstance?* Maybe I would have failed in my abilities in a way that I could never come back from. I tried to make peace with the fate I was given since it seemed to exist for a reason. I could fight with the already existing weapons that I could find and form words from my mouth to try to send a message. There was something within me, though, that kept pulling me away from physically hurting anyone. *Was this the only thing setting me apart from the others?... To be able to say I never killed another being?* I already stood out from the crowd in an embarrassing way by being known as a 'commoner,' why not try to stand out in a way tied to a sense of morality and strong ethics? Maybe I didn't need powers to be able to make a difference. I figured mentally strengthening myself would be the change I needed to make.

"Two women and two men from our group are under attack!" Anon announced as we got closer.

The one who could be seen flying was the man named Kason from our faction. Only the males were given wings in the Over Grounds morphing stages. He was above everyone else trying to attack the rivaling group with the advantage of creating greater distance between them while the other man was firing harpoon shots on the shore. Anon sprung into the air without hesitation to back him up. With blue veins enlarging in his arms, Anon channeled his ability instantly while aiming at those below with fast precision; it was impressive how he seemed to be comfortable with using his powers right away like he already had hours of practice.

"How are you doing Kason?" Anon asked loudly over the sound of weapons being discharged and the ocean beginning to roar.

"As well as can be expected. I'm just glad you showed up!" Kason responded, "I'm having a hard time firing right now. My palms are so sweaty I think my nerves are holding me back."

"That's okay, just look out for the others. I'll try to get a few good hits in." Anon spotted the nearest member of the Oceanic Guardian faction and soared straight towards him.

Gebu and I got behind the man from our group and watched as Anon went partially into the water to grab the stranger in the water. He was trying to entangle Anon with seaweed from his palms, but was disoriented with the loss of air from the tight death grip around his throat. A bolt of lightning travelled through Anon's arm, creating a painful shockwave in the man's neck that traveled throughout his entire body, and his skin began to burn. There was another man that looked similar to him who was close by in the water... he ended up dying from the current too.

"No! You killed Zavier and his brother!" one of his people cried out in distress as the lifeless body began sinking into the ocean.

The woman who spoke came out of the water just enough to strike Anon who was still close by. Her arms were also morphed, and she had what looked to be thousands of stinging cells and multiple tentacles, the same as on a jellyfish. She stung the majority of Anon's right thigh and he wailed out in excruciating pain. Anon flew away from her and back closer to the shore with the rest of us to get away.

The Over Grounds member that Gebu and I were standing closest to was someone who I was not familiar with. He looked at the two of us with confusion. "Why are you both not fighting? What is wrong with you?"

"W-we don't have powers. I mean, I can f-fly, but I can't do much more than that I'm so-sorry." Gebu was stuttering and slurring his words together out of fear.

"Well you both could still at least make yourselves useful." He sighed and handed Gebu the second harpoon rifle he had. "These are the only two I have. You know how to use this, right?"

"Of course." Gebu clearly lied.

"What about you? How do you not have any weapons on you?" he asked me.

"I have one right here." I pulled a boning knife out of my waistband that I had never used before. I had it on me to feel safer and use it for delivering empty threats, but I didn't want to hurt anyone else with it.

"Stop standing around and go help then! Why is Anon the only one pulling any weight around here?" he angrily shouted at us before firing off a harpoon shot at the member who struck Anon. He hit her though she didn't die instantly, but came frantically out of the water and killed him with her spear as blood started to slowly exit her body.

Aside from her arms, she was completely covered in pale scales. She began to shift the water behind her effortlessly with a quick turn of her head. "You should not have crossed us. My name is Elena and I'm going to make sure you don't get to go home now."

She targeted Kason first; his nerves seemed to make him an easy target. I figured that meant Gebu and I would be next. The current she had created surged forward and swept him off of his feet, pulling him over to her and away from the shore.

"Someone help!" Kason called out as he was on his back and being yanked forwards. "I can't get up!"

"That's the idea." Elena took her spear and shoved the rusted blade into his heart as cold sea water rushed past him. "Who's next?"

"Gebu, we have to at least try to fight. We can't die without trying." I almost stuttered on every single word.

"Easy for you to say. I've never even held a harpoon gun before. At least you have a knife to use." Gebu responded.

"How long have you been here and you don't have any real weapons with you?" I asked him with a bewildered expression.

"Now is not the time to start a conversation!" The volume of Gebu's voice raised as Elena made eye contact with him.

"You sure you know how to handle that thing?" she asked him smugly and started closing distance with her bloody spear in hand.

"Leave him alone!" I held onto my knife tightly as I braced myself for an attack.

Elena rolled her eyes and targeted her next shot at me. I was knocked backwards as water went in my eyes and up into my nostrils. My face was burning and I tried to bring myself back up to my feet. Thankfully my weapon was still gripped in my right hand. I could see Anon laying down, struggling from the wound on his leg with two of our women trying to tend to him.

"Ladies please help us over here!" I managed to yell out. "Anon, I'm sorry but you're going to have to wait!"

"Omar help me!" Gebu called out as Elena walked closer to him with her weapon still raised.

Thankfully one of the women, Lyra, didn't hesitate at my request for providing a helping hand. She ran from Anon and came hurtling towards Elena, grabbing on and knocking her to the ground. I had never seen her use her ability before. While kneeling on the woman, she looked up at the sky and put both her hands into the air. While exerting all of her energy, she started to form a gunmetal colored rain cloud up above. *What kind of droplets will come from that?* To her misfortune, she was interrupted by Elena getting the upper hand and flipping her over. I ran over to the two of them and saw this as my opportunity to inflict damage.

"Come on Omar!" our ally said to me as she wrestled our opponent and saw my knife. "What are you waiting for? Stab her!"

The other member was already by my side and was also frustrated by my slow response. Elena screamed and bit into Lyra's nose and lips with her jagged teeth, tearing off a huge chunk of flesh. Lyra wailed in pain and let go of Elena as she rolled around in agony. The Oceanic Guardians had a definite advantage over us Over Grounds in this fight–we were standing at the welcome mat of their own terrain. Elena managed to get up and drove her spear into the gaping hole that was left from her bite.

"I'm sorry but I can't be here for this." Gebu threw the harpoon gun down on the ground and used his inconsequential wings to start flying away.

"You coward!" the other woman in our faction loudly exclaimed. She grabbed the knife out of my hand and ran over to finish the kill. Elena, although badly hurt, wrangled with the knife in her hands and defended herself with her fists and the woman from our group tried to avoid being stung by her upper morphed arms.

"Omar, you need to help her!" Anon tried to get back up as he spoke, still clinging onto the exposed mesh of torn skin and fabric of his wound.

Elena took the combat knife and turned around quick enough to finish off our team member by causing her to run her stomach into the spear. "I did it. I will get to go home. I will be okay."

Anon limped over to me as we both looked at Elena talking to herself. We watched as she finally fully bled out from the harpoon shot from earlier. It must have hit her spine as she seemed to start having a lot of trouble moving one half of her body. She looked up at us and gave an unusual grin.

"Why are you smiling at us?" Anon questioned.

"The stone…" she started to say. "The part of it that's in the ocean…"

"What about the stone?" My interest grew.

"Neither of you have any idea what is coming." Elena coughed as we watched the life leave her eyes.

"What do you think that means?" Anon asked me.

As I looked over at him, I was reminded of his injury. "Let's not worry about it right now. We need to get your leg fixed. Here, grab onto my shoulder and I'll help guide you back to our faction."

Anon limped next to me and we made our way to the platform as the night began coming to a close. Unfortunately, we had just lost many of our healers in the fight. *Wait, we still have a healer.* I remembered Zayika's ability and felt hopeful that we could get help. Even though she hadn't used her power much, we figured she was our only real chance at saving Anon. We found her in her room asleep.

"Zayika." I lightly tapped on her bed frame. "Anon is hurt pretty badly. Could you please help?"

"I'm trying to rest." She groaned and turned onto her other side.

"This is serious. We need you to wake up." Anon said in a sterner tone. It was clear he was in a lot of discomfort by the way he spoke through gritted teeth, but Zayika didn't seem to care. "There was a fight by the ocean and it got really bad. I had my leg stung and torn open."

The two of us didn't let up and hovered over her until she groaned again.

"Fine. I will lose sleep and do this but both of you now owe me favors, just so you know. What kind of trouble are you two getting into out there? I figured you're the type to let the other groups be idiots and have them take care of each other for us." She sprung up and turned her bedside light on. "Anon, take your pants off and sit down."

He did as he was told, pulling the shredded fabric away carefully, I stood nearby and watched anxiously as the healing was about to take place.

"The process may not be very fast, but I'm sure it will be effective. I've never really done this before on someone else so don't blame me if you don't like the results." She became defensive for some reason.

"It's okay. I'm not trying to rush you. I'm just grateful that you can do this for me." Anon smiled but wasn't met with the same energy from her since she huffed at him.

Zayika's skin started to glow from within, especially the palms of her hands. "This feels good." she stated loudly with a bit of a maniacal look. She sat on the edge of her bed, with Anon next to her, and forcefully shoved her hand onto his exposed wound which made him cringe. Her eyelids kept opening further as his skin began melding together quite quickly.

"You're lucky you didn't bleed out somehow." With enlarged eyes, she focused on his face.

"Yeah I definitely am lucky. But hey, who even knows how much blood I have in me anyways after being morphed? Seems like lightning is what's keeping me kicking around." Anon laughed a little.

"That wasn't funny." Zayika said with a straight face then looked downwards at her hand again and noticed that the injury was fully healed. For some reason, though, she kept it on his thigh. Her body looked iridescent as her long nails started to push down into Anon's leg.

"Okay. I think we're done here." he nervously said and tried to move away.

Zayika didn't stop and her hands kept getting brighter. I could even feel some warmth that was being emitted from her body from partly across the room. Her green eyes almost looked as if they were swirling around in their sockets as they were met with Anon's amiable brown ones again.

"Alright knock it off, Zayika." I stepped closer to the two of them. "Seems like you're getting a bit… carried away?"

She rested her face which caused her eyes to return to normal and she let go of him. "Both of you now owe me favors for fixing that." With a hateful glance, she partially shoved Anon off of the bed and flipped herself back underneath her covers.

I went to catch him as he stumbled. "Thanks man." he told me and then went to pick up his pants off from the dusty floor.

"No problem." I replied.

"Get out of here." We both heard Zayika say while laying against a pillow, the top of her silver hair peeking out from the rough blanket that was covering her. "Don't forget about the favors you owe me."

CHAPTER NINE: SPLIT SECOND

Zekiel

Present

I walked away from my conversation last night with Nathaniel feeling enlightened. I also felt hopeful that I might have had a real chance at returning to Earth with Saige. I wanted to be given a second chance in embracing my future. I went inside our faction's walls with a more complete self-perception than I had earlier. I knew that I needed to hold onto my connection with Saige. She was the only one who helped me learn to feel emotions again after the accident. Without a doubt Saige was the one who listened when no one else wanted to or didn't know how to. She always understood that there's more to a person than what originally meets the eye. If it had not been for her... my life would be stuck in time. *Devastation.* I would feel stagnant without her. For some reason the two of us were brought to the planet together. Was that because I wouldn't have enough motivation to fight for my life alone if she wasn't here? Probably.

I woke up early and stood outside for a brief amount of time trying to collect my thoughts. The planet's sunset was much slower than it was back at home. The sun barely showed itself through the thick fog that had gathered during the night. Yellow hues danced out of magenta ones as they were pulled away from each other slowly. Experiencing self-reflection in the face of this twisted and beautiful environment was destined. As the new day approached, I anticipated a small outroar that would inevitably combust once the rest of the faction heard of Nathaniel's news. It was difficult to keep his secrets to myself during the night, I could hardly keep my eyes closed. His message would awake an inner spark of terror in everyone here–the type to ignite dangerous competition to earn the scarce wishes. I had a feeling that the turn of events after his announcement would grow sinister in the worst way possible. What we were told at the ceremony was already bad enough without the odds being cut even thinner. It was only a matter of time before he arrived to get everyone else up to speed with the truth.

I knew that my duty was to protect Saige and keep myself well for us. The past would haunt me every day... I had no way around its disruptive reminders of my last relationship. I had to keep moving forward despite my pain. I was always thankful that I didn't have to do it alone because of Saige. I'm glad I had a friend as great as her. As I made my way back to my assigned room, I saw her leaning up against my door frame. Watching two of the Land Dwellers killed by Nero, their remains having to be washed off of us, was numbingly terrible. We didn't talk much about what happened. Silently the two of us tried to carry on and stay alive.

"Why are you looking at me like that?" she asked with a confused expression. "Surprised I'm up this early?"

"I have some news for you." I took her hand. "Let's go inside the room to discuss this."

I pulled my dusty curtains open and we sat on my bed in the corner of the room as the suspense between us had already started to grow.

"Since when do you have news for me? Is it good or bad?"

"Both in different ways. Do you remember that bunker we stumbled upon when we first got here?"

"Yes, but we haven't been near that area again since then. Why are you asking?"

"Because the man that was sleeping there, his name is Nathaniel, and he is a Land Dweller too."

Saige paused. *She is always good at thinking before she speaks.* "That doesn't make any sense. How can he be one of us? We already have a faction of ten."

"He's an early member of this faction from years ago. He has hidden himself deep within the ground out of sight from the others who are here."

"When did you talk to him?"

"Yesterday and you won't believe what he told me. What the faction representatives told us at the ceremony was a lie. This game that we're in is not a free for all competition in which wishes and tickets home are earned purely through survival. There are only a select few with the calling of carrying a wish and... you're one of them."

Saige's eyes searched around my face for answers. She pulled a leg underneath herself as she sat as if she was bracing for a disappointing twist to my message.

"I'm one of them?"

"Yes, you're called a 'Wish Carrier.' Anon and Omar are too."

"How would Nathaniel know this?"

"Your dreams revealed it all. He overheard your conversation with Anon in the bunker while we all were looting. Those dreams that you guys were talking about were your calling to carry this level of importance."

"What's the difference between you and me then? What about Omar? He didn't have a dream."

"Wishes give someone the opportunity to go home with the ability to change the life they are returning to. Wish Carriers don't have to kill anyone to get a chance, they just have to survive. By default, you, Omar, and Anon already have this gift and are set to return back to Earth. If someone kills a Wish Carrier, then the wish they had will be passed along to the one who murdered them. Omar has no abilities because he was never morphed like us, which apparently makes him important in a messed-up way."

"Wow. This is a lot to process."

"I understand. There is one other thing I should mention though."

Saige's attention starkly shifted to the window behind me. "Hold that thought and look outside. Nathaniel is approaching our front doors. That's him, right? I didn't get the best look at him when he was chasing us, but I don't know who else that could be."

I turned to look and saw Nathaniel walking alone up to our courtyard.

"Yes that's him. He's coming to tell this news to all of the other Land Dwellers." I moved to face her.

"Why is Anon following after him?"

"What? Why would he be here?" I spun around again and this time lifted the latch on the window to hear what was happening below.

Anon flew downwards from the sky above and rattled the ground as he landed. The wind created through the force of his wings knocked the air out of Nathaniel's lungs.

"You're not going to do this. You're going to cause chaos!" Anon yelled ahead of him.

After Nathaniel regained enough of his composure, he lifted himself onto his knees to look at Anon in the eyes. "What are you talking about?"

"Your conniving secrets and tales of the planet's stone. The danger you're willing to put my friends and me in. You're trying to paint targets on our foreheads."

"I have never spoken to you before. How would you know what I'm going to do?"

"I don't have to explain myself to you." Anon's arms began filling with hues of neon blue. His veins were prominent as they pulsated thickly underneath his glowing skin. "You're not getting what you want from me or Omar. In fact, no one from your faction will!"

Anon flew upwards and shot out a sharp ray of lightning through Nathaniel's chest, causing him to instantly scream out in agony. The sound of the shot caused a loud boom, drawing everyone's attention from our faction.

"What is going on?" Saige asked loudly as we ran quickly to get to the front yard. It was already too late by the time we got there to intervene for Nathaniel in any way. A substantial amount of his blood sprayed out behind him as Anon's bolt of light shredded his entire chest apart. Pieces of his ribs and internal organs laid all around him. Anon stopped staring at his dead body and looked up at Saige and me. He had some of Nathaniel's blood falling down the complete lower portion of his twitching face.

"What's going on, Saige, is I just saved mine and Omar's life." He wiped his mouth off with the back of his hand as the electric charge within his arms began to cool down and slowly vanish.

"What's wrong with you Anon? He was a valuable member of my faction." I voiced strongly. "You didn't even know him!"

"Zekiel, in case you haven't realized this yet, which would be astonishing if you haven't, we are supposed to fight to stay alive here. I have a home I'm trying to get back to and I'm not afraid to make sacrifices to do so." Anon responded. "I'm especially not afraid to make them to protect my own. I heard the conversation that you had with Nathaniel yesterday and I knew I needed to put a stop to what was going to happen next."

"You have no right listening in on others' conversations. Who says that I won't share the same information that he did with me to all of the other Land Dwellers? Do you really believe I have no loyalty to my own faction?" I asked.

Anon stood silently. He looked at Saige for a moment and then back at me. He began lowering himself down onto the ground and sat next to Nathaniel's broken remains. He kept his eyes away from the image of his destruction. "Killing him was something that I had to do. Yeah, I didn't know him, okay? That was different than me harming either of you. What I just did was in self-defense. How would I know if he would hunt me down to steal my wish and take down Omar for one too while he was at it? He was going to send all of you directly to the two of us. There is no fairness in that. You can't blame me."

"He was a Land Dweller and so are we. Why do you think that Saige and I won't eliminate you, especially after what you just did?"

"Aren't we friends? We could find a way to all go home. The six of us from the start can all group up again. We can find a loophole to these wishes and have you, Amira, and Zayika saved too. We have to stay loyal to each other." Anon said desperately.

I tapped on Saige's shoulder and nodded for her to walk away with me.

"Anon you are right that we arrived on this planet at the same time, but unfortunately your correctness stops there. We traveled together for a short while after that but were separated and given our own people to protect. My only loyalties are to Saige and to the other Land Dwellers now. You should leave. I make no promise to not kill you the next time we meet."

A small pool of tears started to fill up Anon's dark brown eyes as Saige and I left him on the ground.

Five Years Before

"I can't believe that this happened." Saige said to Zekiel, still being embraced in his arms. "If there's anything I can ever do for you Zeek, you know you can count on me to help. It's hard for me to even find what to say. I'm so sorry."

He nodded next to her and inhaled deeply. "There's nothing that can be done now. Jasmine is just... gone. Saige, I feel so broken."

She made enough distance between them to look up at him. With her cotton sleeve covering her hand, she wiped away the tears that had fallen completely down his face. "I'm here. You're not alone and you're never going to be." She pushed the blonde strands of hair that were covering his eyes back behind his ears as she looked at his sorrowful expression.

"I don't want to ever lose you. I don't think you understand how much you mean to me. I can't lose you too. You're the truest friend I've ever had. I don't know what I'd do without you." He couldn't look directly into her eyes.

Saige felt his heart rate increase and noticed his face flush red. She tried to calm him down. "You won't lose me, I wouldn't let that happen. I can't lose you either. We'll always be there for one another. I'll make sure I look after you for Jasmine."

Present

As Saige and I started to make our way back inside, another Land Dweller named Draydon approached us with several questions as Fabian was behind him following close by.

"We heard all of the noise, what happened?" He looked behind me and saw the gory mess spread along the ground. "Who died?"

"Nathaniel!" I responded. "The man you saw yesterday briefly before he pulled me aside to talk."

"Who killed him?" Draydon started running over to Nathaniel's shattered body.

"I did." Anon, who was still on the ground but a fit farther away, answered him.

"You shall pay for this! How dare you kill one of ours." Draydon started to craft a land-built pistol with his hand, creating it from the rubble and materials below him.

"I don't want any trouble! I was just leaving." Anon got up swiftly and started to fly into the air again.

"You're not getting off that easy!" A shot rang out as Anon ducked underneath it. "A kill for a kill!"

Anon sent out a bolt of lightning from his palm down in front of Draydon, using just enough force to stun him backwards. "I don't want to kill you!"

"You seemed to have no trouble murdering one of our own!" Fabian began preparing his ability of crafting grenades. I watched on as the two of our remaining people began aiming at Anon. Saige stood beside me, watching my reaction closely.

"Should we do something?" she asked me.

"Why would we Saige? People should pay for their reckless actions. The driver who hit my girlfriend better have paid and anyone else who has caused premeditated, or even accidental, harm to another being needs to pay." It felt like my face was melting off as I spoke. My adrenaline spiked as I watched my people terrorize my former friend. I felt my fists tightening up with a clenched jaw.

Anon's vast dark wings launched him further into the sky as he directed himself towards his faction's terrain. "I had to do what I did!" he stated loudly as he flew away.

"I want his wish." I whispered under my breath to myself. Saige already had one so as long as she stayed alive, she was set to go back to Earth. All I needed was one wish to do the same. I wanted a wish. I needed to kill Anon. I had to make him pay for what he did.

All of us Land Dwellers made our way back inside. The four of us felt sick and distressed after losing Nathaniel. There was clearly a life that needed to be avenged and we all knew this. Saige and I talked for what felt like hours about what we should do. We wasted precious daylight going back and forth exercising our options. She didn't want to hunt and kill, but I got to a point where I did, and I almost hated myself for that. I tried to explain to her why I needed to be the one to make the decision about dealing with Anon. It felt as though a festering rage within me had been unleashed. I was sick of people getting away with destroying others. I wanted revenge and closure, and felt as though I wouldn't get one without the other.

Fabian and Draydon tried to ask me what Nathaniel told me the night before and wanted to know why Anon set out to kill him in the first place. They wanted to strategize and come up with a calculated plan, but I couldn't bring myself to share the details that I had learned with anyone. My anger turned to silence and it started to scare them. All I could think about was getting Anon's wish. The day felt like it was a rug tugged out from under all of our feet as it seamlessly turned into night. I decided to not waste any more time and went off to my room to prepare for my confrontation with Anon.

"I'm going after him. Saige, you're staying here."

"Zekiel, let me come with you. It isn't fair to not let me help." Saige sat in the corner, looking helpless as I packed up a few of my belongings in a woven sack to throw over my shoulder.

"I know you're smarter than what you're saying right now. You know why you can't join me. We need to try to keep you safe as much as we can. Having you walk up to the front doors of a rivaling faction is one of the worst decisions we could make." I walked over to her and put my hand lightly against the side of her face. "Be patient here and hold onto that wish for us, okay?"

She put her hand on top of mine and shook her head. "You frustrate me."

"I know. It's important that I do." I forced a half-hearted smile and checked outside the window to make sure no one was nearby outside. Nightfall had visited us too quickly and made it much harder to see.

"How are you going to get up there? You know they have a platform and you don't have the ability to activate it."

"That's why I'm using these." I showed her the handmade harpoon grappling hooks for the rocks. "The others won't care that I'm borrowing them. I'm killing Anon for all of us, not just myself."

"You are doing it for yourself though, Zekiel, because there's not going to be enough wishes for all of us to go home. I won't tell them this though. You know I'm on your side. I hope you get that wish." Saige stood up to give me a tight hug. "We can go on to build a new life together. We can decide to finally be free from the past."

"Exactly. You know that I will do everything in my power to make that come true." I gave her one last look of admiration before I began following my plan underneath cloud-covered stars.

When I finally approached the Over Grounds faction, I was amazed by how much higher it was compared to the view from a distance. The climb and elevation would be a long and difficult one, but the promise of a newfound life garnered far more than enough motivation for me to complete my mission. Hooking the rock successfully and keeping track of the rope wasn't the hardest part. I had to make sure to not look down, which was the most challenging things of all. One glimpse of the planet's grounds from up above was enough to cause intense vertigo throughout my body. I felt as though the journey would never end as several chill winds swept past me. As I got closer to the edge of the platform, I let out a deep breath. My knees were sore from bracing myself and my lungs almost felt frozen. I pulled myself up painstakingly as the edge of rock dug into my stomach and elbows.

Their faction was right in front of me sleeping soundly. I crouched as I surveyed the area and searched for an opening that I could climb through. A partially opened window caught my eye from the right corner of the building and I cautiously entered it. The room I went into was dark and there was someone sleeping on a bed to the left of me. I snuck through the doorway, not knowing who was there. I found myself in their hallway and saw a small row of doors on either side of me. I stepped slowly as I progressed forwards. There was a faint sound at the end in one of the last rooms. I made my way over to it and steadily leaned onto the wall. I could hear Anon, Omar and... Nero? *Not this guy.* I fully realized he was placed into the same team as my previous friends.

"Just go back to your own room, Nero. I need to have a talk with Omar." I heard Anon say hastily. "Maybe you can convince Zayika to heal your wound, I don't think her ability is capable of giving you your wing back though."

"I can't fly now so this ultimately sucks. Those tree people are savages, don't let them get close to your wings. I'm not leaving until you tell me what happened down on the ground." Nero responded and then I heard him take a drink. "Plus, I don't need Zayika's help. You're delusional, I'll be fine. Screw her anyways–she always has a bad attitude."

"So do you." Anon scoffed. "Plus why are you even drinking in here? Go to your own room. It's not your business what happened back there, and I need to have a private conversation."

"Why do you have scratch marks on your skin? You seemed exhausted when you got back up here. It also looks like there was blood on your face, did you finally use your abilities too? It's fun, isn't it?"

"Nero, I said you need to leave. Come on. I'm not answering your questions."

"Hey you should be thankful that someone is showing an interest in your life. Let me guess, not used to having that back at home?"

"Just leave." Omar finally spoke up.

I shifted my weight to my other leg as I kept listening in the shadows.

"We're supposed to be teammates, guys!" I could tell by the sound of his voice that Nero walked closer to the door. "Wait–do you guys hear something?"

I held my breath for a few moments. The wooden floors were awful for sneaking on.

"Nero don't you have someone else to be annoying right now? Or some girl to scare off?" Anon opened the door for him. "Just go. We will see you in the morning for breakfast."

"Man, you guys try to act tough for honestly being the weakest links of this entire faction. Not even one kill exists between the two of you combined, that's embarrassing." Nero started walking into the hallway holding a candle. Thankfully, I moved out of view quick enough behind a corner wall. "What a shame that you were given the most powerful wings, Anon, too bad they'll never be used properly. If I had those wings, I would be completely unstoppable."

"No one cares about you, Nero. Read the room. It's not your business if we've attacked anyone or not." Anon shut the door and Nero made his way down the opposite side from where I was standing.

I got closer to the door when he was gone and listened in on the conversation as the two resumed talking. "That guy needs to be put in his place." Omar laughed. "How did he already lose a wing as fast as he did? He sure likes to run his mouth and it gets him into trouble."

"Why couldn't he have been in a different faction?" Anon responded.

"Alright enough about him. You needed to talk to me? What's going on?" Omar's voice consistently sounded concerned whenever he would talk.

"Something happened earlier today."

"Did you get hurt? It looks pretty obvious that you got into a fight."

"I'm okay, well, in some ways I am. Physically, I'm put together but my mental state seems to be a different story. Ever since we heard the truth of what's going on here... I haven't been able to shake the feeling I have."

I waited patiently for Anon to reveal the news of the murder that he committed to Omar. This was my golden chance to avenge Nathaniel's death by taking Anon's life. Receiving a wish from him was the ultimate goal. I would most likely have to take Omar's life too since he would be involved, which would mean two wishes, but I wasn't complaining. My thoughts were interrupted by footsteps coming from the hall. I stayed in hiding, frustrated that someone was coming near. I got a quick look around the corner and saw Nero walking with Zayika. He must've told her that there was a serious conversation taking place between Anon and Omar and she wanted to listen in too. I could tell that they were whispering as the two of them quietly stood at a doorway near me, all three of us concealed from view.

"What's wrong with your head? Mentally, what's going on?"

"Omar, I need to tell you that I murdered someone today. There's no simple or better way to state that."

There was silence for what felt like minutes.

"You murdered a person?"

"Yes, but it was self-defense, okay?" Anon's voice started to shake slightly.

"Who, when... why did you do this? Do you know what this means? You took a person's life!" I could hear Omar's feet hit the ground as he, I assumed, jumped off from his bed or chair that he had been on.

"Hey, don't make me feel worse than I already do. I didn't take happiness or sick pleasure in it, I didn't want to do it at all okay? But I knew I had to kill him to stay alive and to protect you too."

"Don't tell me you killed the older Land Dweller?"

"Nathaniel."

"I don't know what to say to you."

"Omar, he knew stuff about us that even we didn't know! He was on his way to tell all of the Land Dwellers that you, Saige, and I have wishes. Plus, who is to say that Saige would still be safe from her own group? It would have only been a matter of time before we were tracked down and murdered in our sleep right after her."

"Anon you can't solve problems with violence and killing. I don't think they would kill her. Some people have morals, you know that right?"

"There's only Zekiel, Saige, and I believe two other men left in their faction from what I could count when I was there. It looked like they've lost a lot of their people already. Since she already has a wish, they would definitely come after ours! Me killing Nathaniel was a favor for us both."

"We have to be better than this and not forget where we came from." Omar said.

"I haven't forgotten where I came from!" Anon stood up loudly also, "The only reason why I did what I chose was so that I could make it back to where I came from! I had to protect myself. You need to realize how valuable we are on this planet!"

I could hear Nero and Zayika muttering more words to one another again but faster than before. This was the first they were hearing of this news.

"This isn't okay. What you did is not okay. This will follow you for forever Anon."

"Look. I know I'm assigned to this faction, but my loyalties lie with you and the rest of our original group, the six of us. Nathaniel was someone I had no ties to and no connection with. He was going to put us in horrific danger. At least this way we can try to stay under the radar long enough to survive until the end of this sick game."

I then heard excitement in Nero's voice from around the corner. "Zayika, if what Anon is saying is true? Then that means Saige can be our way off this planet, well, if we only get a wish from eliminating someone that's from a different faction."

"Yeah she is. She's only one person, though. Which one of us will kill her?"

"I guess whoever gets there first." I could practically hear the wicked smile on his face. "I mean, no disrespect to you because I do think you can fight, but I don't know if you have a bias towards her like the two weaklings in there do."

"Nero, I'm here to survive. I'm willing to do what it takes." Zayika said with a sinister voice. "You should know that people like us have no limits."

"Okay so be it. Let the best one win." he responded. "I'm ready to get a wish secured tonight."

"Why not wait until tomorrow? Until daylight?" she said.

"I don't have an interest in sitting around and losing my opportunity to kill her. If you want to wait, then that's on you. I'm going to go grab my throwing knives." Nero took off down the hallway.

I knew I only had a short amount of time to get to Saige before he did. I started to make my way out of the hiding spot that I was in. Very carefully I attempted to stand up completely without making any noise. Because of my nerves I failed at this and jerked my hand too roughly against the wall.

"Are there people listening to us in the hallway?" I heard Anon ask. "This information really can't be spread, it will only cause problems."

"Let me follow whoever it is and make sure nothing bad happens. Just stay here and please try to get some rest." Omar told him.

I hurried off to Saige by venturing back into the night. I had to safely maneuver the cliff again and get down to the ground. Adrenaline kicked in and sharpened my senses, resulting in me getting to the bottom faster than it took to get up there. Thankfully Nero couldn't fly so I got a head start. I began sprinting along the dirt until I reached the jungle, anxious to return to her. I felt a stab of regret after thinking that I should have taken her with me like she had asked.

CHAPTER TEN: BARBAROUS CRUELTY

Saige

Present

Waiting for Zekiel to return from visiting the Over Grounds faction had felt like a lifetime. All I wanted was to see his face again, hug him, and hold onto him for as long as I could. I was rooting for us to make it. I believed that we would make it back home together and live a long life with the other by our side. I felt like there was a lot I needed to say to him even though I was near him often. Up until being taken to the planet, it never seemed as though it was the right time to share with him how I felt. My feelings ran deep, deeper than the undiscovered parts of the ocean, and I knew that I wouldn't be able to get rid of them. I didn't know if he also felt the same way about me. What I did know was that our lives were truly in danger and that I may never have another chance to tell him the truth if something was to go wrong. I needed to see him again. The four walls of the room I was in started to crowd around me, so much to the point where I could have sworn they were moving closer to one another. *Is he okay? Did anything happen? Has... Anon killed him first?*

I tapped my fingers against the wooden wall in front of me until there was a soft knock on my bedroom door. I knew it wasn't Zekiel, he wouldn't have been back so soon. Although I felt at ease knowing that the odds of it being someone who wasn't from our faction were slim, so I let out the breath I had started holding.

"Can I come in?" I heard a man say.

"Who is it?"

"Fabian." He knocked again. "This is kind of important."

I opened the door and was greeted by the man with tall shoulders who introduced us to our new people. He had a long untamed beard that reached his faded shirt and was shaking his foot up and down hurriedly. I stepped out from my room and talked to him with caution.

"What's important?" I asked with wide eyes.

"Draydon and I have been talking about you and Zekiel, your... partner. We like you both as people but not how you have been acting. We're getting the feeling that there's things you know that you aren't sharing with us."

"What makes you feel that way?" *Act naive. Of course there would be things the two of us wouldn't share with others.*

"I was there when Nathaniel first approached the faction. He seemed like a kind man with a lot of knowledge. Although something seemed off when he took Zekiel aside privately away from everyone else." Fabian looked at me intensely.

"He did? I wasn't there when that happened."

"Come on, don't act innocent. You two clearly are hiding something."

I stayed silent as I thought about how to approach the conversation. "What would we be hiding?"

"I'm not sure but it was enough for Zekiel to hardly look at any of us earlier when we were asking him questions before he took off into the night. We did notice, though, that he only talked to you."

"That's because we are close. We knew each other before we even arrived at this planet. Look, maybe it doesn't seem like it, but we are a part of this faction and we do want to belong to this group. Us talking privately wasn't an attempt to exclude anybody."

"All I know is that I saw him escape not too long ago and he looked as though he was running on borrowed time, it sent a chill over my skin. Where is he going?"

I have to lie... at least to an extent.

"He went to kill some people, okay? From the Over Grounds and Oceanic Guardian factions. You remember what was said at the opening ceremony–the last group standing gets to go home. Well, none of us will ever get back to Earth if we hide out in these buildings every day and night. Some of us have to get our hands dirty in order to shave the numbers down."

"Why wouldn't he tell us this? We understand that fighting is the integral part of survival here. I'd be willing to kill with him."

"Then you can go off and do it yourself then. He wanted to go alone because he's kind of a lone wolf."

"I've seen the bond you two have. A lone wolf doesn't have someone like you by their side." Fabian rolled his shoulders and sighed. "Why wouldn't he take you with him?"

"He didn't want me to get hurt." I responded. *This wasn't a lie.*

"Well that's the only thing you've said that's made sense to me so far. I don't know, I've just sort of felt like Zekiel's kind of our leader around here. With him gone, I guess it's on me to make the tough calls. Our group is doing awful if you can't tell. Besides you two... Draydon and I are the only ones left out of the original ten."

"Yeah. The rest weren't so lucky."

"That's an understatement. I heard that three of our own were eaten by an anglerfish."

I couldn't help but let out a laugh. "An anglerfish? You have to be joking. How is that even possible?"

"How is this place and us being morphed even possible?"

"Fair enough."

"I'll go talk to Draydon and see if he's up for fighting with me. You're right. We all can't sit around and wait for action to take place, we have to make it happen. Him and I can go look for Zekiel."

"No!" I said too loudly. "You don't have to do that. He can take care of himself."

"Sure, but Draydon hardly can and how well will I be able to look after myself if I'm babysitting him?"

I shrugged. "Do what you want, just please leave Zekiel out of it."

"I really don't understand you both." Fabian said as he turned around and walked away from me.

I let out another breath that I had been holding in for a while. I always had a tendency to hold my breath when I would think too much. My stomach felt as though it was in knots as I stepped back into my room.

Two Years Before

Saige headed through the post office's glass front doors with an off-white colored envelope in her hands.

She went over to the line of others and anxiously awaited her turn. When it was time, she took a deep breath and considered leaving instead of delivering her message.

"Are you coming up here or what?" the postal worker practically shouted. "There are other people who want to get on with their day and you're holding them up."

Saige's glossed over look was replaced by her eyes widening in embarrassment. "I'm so sorry, there was something I was distracted by."

"I don't care to hear your story. I just want to ship off whatever it is you've brought here." he grumbled as he examined the chipping paint in his cubicle.

"Okay I have a letter to send."

"You seem nervous about dropping it off here." he stated.

"After this stop I won't be heading back home or else I would have just put it in my personal mailbox. I have somewhere I need to go, but there's someone who needs to read what is in this." She handed him the envelope with a shaky hand.

"Why do you think I want to hear all of this? It's weird enough that you're sending a handwritten note anyways. Do you know what year it is?"

"Yes I do. I think it's sentimental to write something handwritten and I know he will appreciate it."

"So is this your love letter to some guy?"

"No, what we have is not like that. There's no romance between us."

The employee smirked. "I mean if you have to say there's 'no romance,' it makes it seem like you're trying to convince your own self that there isn't."

Saige held back a smile. "I mean, we'll see, hopefully I'm wrong. Maybe I do have a chance."

Present

The thought of Zekiel leaving our safe terrain to hunt down Anon burdened my mind. I paced around my room for a while waiting for him to get back. *I can't lose him.* As time continued slipping away, I grew worried that something had put him in harm's way. Zekiel could defend himself well, but he was walking straight onto the enemy's grounds. There were several numbers against him and I felt a panic coming over me at the thought. *Why didn't I just go with him... What if he actually wanted me to?* I couldn't sit still any longer and wait for a seemingly inevitable demise. I got up from my bed and armed myself with my knife secured to the belt along my waistline. It was chilling to step outside. I went out of the back door to not draw any attention to myself from the others, especially Fabian since he was already keeping an eye on me. I walked for a little while before noticing a figure heading in my direction. I leaned onto a tree and waited for them to come closer before making any noise or sudden movements.

"Saige, if you're out there, it's Zekiel." a whisper said.

I felt my tensed muscles relax as I moved toward his voice. "Zeek I'm glad you're safe." I got close enough to touch him and wrapped my arms over his shoulders.

"We won't be safe for long if we don't get back inside. We can't be out in the open like this."

"What happened? Did you kill Anon?"

"No I didn't get the chance to and I can explain more inside. For now, let's just go take cover so we can make a plan. Besides, I told you to wait for me. Why are you putting yourself into danger like this?"

I thought about the last interaction I had with Zekiel before we both were taken to the planet. *I wish I told him the entire truth in that letter.* I realized that I still had time to tell him how I felt.

"You remember the letter I wrote you, right? You remember what it said?" I made myself say what I needed to.

Zekiel inhaled sharply. His eyes looked as though they started to fill with tears as he jerked his head away. "Yeah. I remember."

It felt like there was a huge gap of space between the two of us even though we were standing close to the other. "Zeek, I didn't tell you the entire truth on that piece of paper and I think you already know that."

He gave me an expression I had never seen him do before. He looked... guilty. With a half-hearted smirk, he put his head down, letting his hair fall over his face. I went to put my hand on his chest and he stepped backwards. *What is it?* Normally he would let me touch him. A ray of the moonlight bounced off of his skin, illuminating all of the features he had that I adored.

"Don't say what you're feeling, Saige." He kept his eyes covered partially and refused to look back at me. "Please. Don't make it worse."

"Make what worse?" I hated how desperate I sounded.

"You're a great friend to me and I don't want that ruined." he responded, sounding like he was rushing to get the words out once he started speaking.

"That won't be ruined. How could it be?" It felt like the jungle was listening to our words.

"Your face says it all. You don't even need to tell me what was missing from that letter in words because it's always been written inside of your eyes." Zekiel finally stopped slouching and the next thing he said made my heart feel broken, "I'm sorry if I gave you the wrong idea. It's never been that way for me... about you."

Suddenly, there was the sharp sound of a tree branch snapping and the sound echoed eerily. We both exchanged glances and Zekiel nodded, hinting that he would go ahead and take a look. I stayed still for a moment as he gestured his arm to keep me behind him. Tears were welling in my eyes and I tried to make them stop.

"Who is there?" Zekiel asked bravely. "We are from the Land Dwellers faction and we aren't afraid to fight. Show yourself. I'm sure we have the same motives here."

Nero's slender figure stepped out of the shadows swiftly and he started clapping. "You have no idea what my motives are. That was a great show, by the way." He smiled mischievously at both of us. I looked below his growing grin and saw that his clothes were torn and both of his hands had dried blood on them. As he started to walk closer to us, I noticed that he still had one wing that was also drenched in blood splatter. "Based on that last conversation you both just had though, I'd say the two of you definitely don't have the same motives. It's sad, really. She can't get her hands off of you and you don't have the decency to even look her in the eye. Major yikes."

"Leave us alone." Zekiel demanded.

"Guys, come on, lighten up! It's been awhile since we've seen each other! But this will be the second and last time we cross paths since I plan on slicing you both open in a minute here." His eyes grew wider with each word. "I already have four kills under my belt, which is impressive. You both are impressed right? Those three other tree huggers stood no chance. I actually got to kill a fish freak named Enya since you last saw me. Mermaids are ridiculous, I'm glad I didn't get stuck in that poor excuse of a faction."

"You're bold if you think you can take both of us down. It looks to me that you're barely hanging on as it is." Zekiel stood up taller. "Saylor really did a number on you, didn't she?"

Nero rolled his eyes and started using his power against us again. "I'd say her choking on her own blood and spit doesn't count as a 'number on me,' but to each their own, I guess?"

A whirlpool of wind began spiraling around Zekiel and me and we were forced with our backs against one another. We always had each other's backs. *We just have to stand tall and defend ourselves.*

"You're an irresponsible coward!" I shouted out.

"You might want to be more careful before you speak, you invisible nobody. Look who already has the upper hand. Now it's time for you both to die because there has been enough dialogue. I'm ready to go home!" Nero's voice roared like thunder as he began charging towards the two of us.

"Wait!" Omar's voice rang out from a distance.

Nero stopped running, "What is wrong with you Omar? You're such a walking cliché!" he shouted at him. "What is it now? Can you not see that I'm busy doing what you are too scared to do?" He kept the whirlpool spinning and simultaneously blew a strong gust of wind towards Omar's direction, sending him back first onto a nearby tree.

"Ow! What is wrong with you? We don't have to solve our problems through murder! Let's be better than this. These two are my friends!" Omar said with a strained voice as he hunched over in discomfort. "I met them when I first arrived here. Even though we've been told to kill one another, it doesn't mean that we have to follow twisted rules that break our humanity."

"All you do is talk." Nero scoffed. "You can't make one tough call even if it would save your life. Why can't you get this through your head? Killing is the only option here. It's all about becoming the ultimate survivor now, which means making sacrifices. In case you missed the obvious plotline, being humane doesn't really matter anymore. All of us would hardly be considered human anyways since being morphed. You know what Omar? Maybe you can't understand what I'm saying because you are so painfully ordinary that not even the monsters on this planet wanted to give you a single power... go complain to them about it."

Omar's hopeful expression faded as he looked down at his feet with crossed arms. Luck wasn't ever on his side. It hadn't been, not even since I first met him on the hills. He always seemed to be kicked when he was already down. I've never known what that was like–to feel so alone. *Hopefully Omar will find a true friend or a lover one day, maybe even someone who is both to him... that would make him luckier than me.* He didn't respond to Nero and I didn't blame him.

"That's what I thought. At least one of us has been able to shut you up. I'm tired of hearing you interject about world peace or whatever it is you care about. Now can the extras stop interrupting the action? Back to what I was doing." Nero caused the whirlpool to come to a halt and I dizzily watched as he promptly pulled a throwing knife out of his pocket and aimed it at Zekiel's head.

Time seemed to move in slow motion from that moment on. I went invisible so that I wouldn't be stopped and stood in front of Zekiel, the love of my life, resulting in the rusty blade crashing against my nose, mouth, and between my eyes. Pain filled every ounce of feeling I had as hot blood began pouring everywhere.

"Her wish is mine!" Nero screaming insanely was the last thing that I heard as I fell to the ground. "I knew I would get what I want!"

CHAPTER ELEVEN: NIGHT VANISH

Zayika

Present

After Nero left to go seek out Saige, I knew I couldn't sit by and wait for her wish to be stolen by him. He was definitely a competitor that I was up against. The life I wanted to return to was just as valuable as everyone else's was. I wanted my fair chance to return home. When Nero left, I went to my room to think over my decision. I wanted to head out the next morning, but I knew time wasn't on my side. I needed to follow Nero if I wanted any possibility at all to get Saige's wish. I found some weapons from our faction to take with me even though I was only focused on trying out my power. As I started to leave our building, Anon heard my footsteps and stopped me to ask questions.

"Where are you going?"

"I'm going out, Anon. I have something I need to do."

His expression grew concerned. "Wait, you heard my conversation with Omar, didn't you? That means you know about..."

"Saige. Yes, I know she's a Wish Carrier. I'm going to take her wish and you aren't going to stop me."

"Who do you think I am? Omar? Zayika, I won't judge you for what you need to do. I already have a wish so I don't have a right to critique your choices. Honestly if I didn't have one then I would be in the same shoes as you." Anon continued, "I thought Saige and Zekiel were allies to me, you know, the six of us that started surviving here together? Apparently they don't feel the same way. Your choices are your own. I won't intervene."

"Anon, if you, Omar, and Saige have the wish to take you home then that means there are only three in total. There are ten individuals assigned to each of these three factions. Thirty people fighting for three wishes. You aren't my favorite person here but at least you understand why we need to defend ourselves. I heard Omar lecturing you about what you did. I get that he doesn't have any powers, but it makes him seem to think he has to be everyone's moral compass. Morality is six feet under here." I walked past Anon. "I'll be back, and I will come back with a wish."

He titled his head in bittersweet agreement at me and I made my way to follow Nero. The platform took me down to the ground, which felt like a lifetime. A chance was approaching for me to prove myself, to try out my capabilities on someone else. Everything was thrilling and the jungle was frightening when I approached it. The moon and stars shone in the sky and a light fog fell over all of the trees and vines. In an unnatural way I loved the adrenaline rush of traveling to fight on the planet. I found myself starting to seek the danger and impending doom that was coming for the fate of many. I was getting ready to kill and see my ability in true action. I wanted others to start to fear me. I wanted to come out victorious with a wish and I knew exactly what I would use it for back on Earth. While on my way, I heard a blood curdling scream tear through the silence of the night... I knew it was Zekiel. My heart was pounding with each carefully placed step I took as I followed his echoes. His hollering could only have meant one thing: *Nero definitely got to Saige before me.*

Three Months Before

"I'm not waiting around for them any longer." Zayika proclaimed hastily while using her phone to track down the location of their friends.

"Maybe something else came up that we don't know about. Let's just hangout, only us two. We can't let them ruin the entire night." Andrea responded.

"No, they're wrong so let's go." Zayika grabbed her car keys and quickly made her way to the slippery driveway. The rain wasn't letting up. Andrea followed the pathway to the passenger seat. "Where are we going?"

"To teach them a lesson." The vehicle started up as both of them closed their doors.

"What does that mean? We should leave them alone and enjoy the party together. We don't need the rest of them in order to have fun."

"You don't understand why I care. They did something to me." Zayika began driving and following her smartphone's GPS through the night. "They've been blackmailing me with personal information they accidentally learned."

"What happened?"

"I stole some money, okay?" Zayika kept her eyes ahead of her as they soared through a road filled with fading green streetlights.

Andrea wasn't too shocked. "For what?"

"It doesn't matter anymore what it was for. They have opened themselves up to some problems by not showing up to this party." Her friend's expression demanded more information. "Ugh, look, they found out about money I took from work. They don't know the reason why I did but that wasn't keeping them from attempting to destroy my career. They have been blackmailing me ever since they found out."

"So that's why you've been acting tense… I assumed it was because there were some problems at home."

"Of course there is Andrea. When am I not having home-related problems? But this time, somehow, my problems are even worse."

"So what exactly does the party have to do with them knowing your secret?"

"They were supposed to bring me something tonight, something extremely important. Them not arriving is a silent message sent of unfortunate rejection."

"What are you going to say to them? Whose house are we going to? I think you need to calm down a bit."

"Don't you dare tell me to calm down." Zayika spouted out. "You don't want to be on my hit list too."

Present

"How could you do this?" I watched Zekiel shout as he sobbed.

"How could I do what I'm literally supposed to do here? That seems like an obvious answer to an unnecessary question." Nero replied. "Oh look, here comes Zayika. Hey! I got the kill!" he cheered with celebratory hand gestures and a handsome grin.

Omar had both his hands covering his face and Zekiel was holding Saige's dead body. He stroked her bloody cheek with his finger. A large throwing knife had caved Saige's entire face inwards–the sight of it didn't even phase me.

"You will pay for this Nero." Zekiel's sadness quickly turned to rage. "You are a parasite to this planet!"

Nero started laughing with a demented look in his eyes. "I'm a 'parasite to this planet'? It's a good thing that I'm getting off of it now, isn't it? Looks like you're stuck here!" He put his hand under his chin and pretended to look at an imaginary watch on his other wrist. "Oh wait I forgot I have something scheduled to do right now."

Zekiel's fists tightened. "What are you talking about?"

"Nothing that important–just killing you, too." Nero sneered. "Look, I have two people from my faction here to help me. Come on losers! Zayika it's time for you to do whatever it is you do, and Omar... oh wait I forgot that you're useless. Never mind, I'll take the broken tree giant out by myself."

Nero lifted his hands to begin controlling the wind again and Zekiel managed to spring past the whirlpool that was forming.

"You deserve to lose!" Zekiel punched Nero precisely in the face.

Nero took a step backwards and clutched his nose. "You can land a punch, I will give you that, but your fists are no match for my throwing knives! Just ask your dead girlfriend over there. Oh wait! I mean your wannabe girlfriend... you didn't love her back, did you?"

"You have no idea how heavy the weight of your words are." Zekiel grabbed Nero's throat and lifted him up into the air before he could get a hold of his weapon. "You're not of much use with only one wing, are you?" he said in a mocking tone.

"Screw off, tree hugger." Nero spit in his face.

"You both are fighting too much. Please end this before it gets worse." Omar interjected.

Zekiel, still holding Nero, turned to look at Omar. "Saige dying signed Nero's death warrant. It doesn't get much worse than this." In one swift movement, he reached around and grabbed onto the remaining wing on Nero's back.

"Stop!" Nero winced in agony, the fresh wound on his back from his other wing's previous removal started to tear open further and burn as Zekiel's palms lit up in flames.

"Now you aren't so tough." He yanked downwards on the tattered white feathers with as much force as he could with a surprising amount of strength.

Nero's blood started spouting out of his back as he bit down completely through his own tongue. The last wing was torn out of his back and with melting skin, he bellowed in agony. "You don't understand what you just did!" His words were muffled due to the teeth marks and torn flesh that he had inflicted in his own mouth.

A warp in the air emerged and a spinning black hole formed behind Nero. It acted like a giant vacuum that was attracting and pulling in the air, dirt, and fallen leaves around it. I watched on in disbelief as Nero's skin became fully covered in bubbling sores.

"What do you mean by that?" Zekiel asked as he threw Nero to the ground.

"An eternity sentence for us with wings. You can call me a parasite, but you're a fool if you think I care what words you choose to say. I was only fulfilling my duty to kill here and win this game. Now you've stripped everything from me!"

"I-I don't understand."

Nero's eyes boiled over with resentment as he started to get pulled in. "My mind will be trapped here forever." Zekiel tried to turn away and run but Nero grabbed the back of his long hair. "Your mind will be trapped here too. You will pay for this Zekiel!"

Within an instant, the two of them vanished seemingly into thin air, falling into the mystifying passageway behind them. The silence seemed so loud once they disappeared. *Where did they go?* Omar and I tried to process everything that just happened.

"Nero said 'eternity sentence'? Do you know anything about that?" I looked over at my shaken-up acquaintance.

"I don't know much, but Gebu told Anon and me that when a man from our faction loses both wings... they're tormented forever. A fate worse than death. Nero will apparently be lost in a void and he took Zekiel right along with him. That portal looked like it went straight into nothingness."

I felt sadistically intrigued by everything that he said. "Wow. That's brutal. Nero really didn't give a damn about anyone but himself, did he?"

"No and it makes me sick to my stomach." Omar said but I silently disagreed because I could see where Nero was coming from.

"I see Saige was killed too. A knife to the face seems like a painful way to go." I bent over her body; her face was unrecognizable.

"Yeah, she bled out." Omar looked like he was going to throw up any second. "I don't think I will ever get the mental image of it happening out of my head. There was a crunching sound... and it–" He actually gagged.

"Don't hurt yourself by giving me the details." I stood up. *He has a much weaker stomach than me.* "I guess it's sad that she's gone." *No–it is only sad that I did not get her wish.*

"I hope at least Amira is okay out there. Anon probably knows how she is doing."

"How would he know that?" I flipped around on the ball of my foot.

"They've really become close friends."

"She's supposed to be the enemy."

"Well... they still meet up with one another." Omar tried to defend them.

"I knew that they did that earlier, but not since we've been told to fight one another."

"If you believe what we are told to believe then yes, she is, but you don't have to make others your enemies if you think for yourself. You decide how you're going to react to your own environment."

"Omar, enemies exist here, okay?" I found myself getting oddly defensive.

Something about Anon had started to get under my skin, even more than Omar's constant morality checkups on everyone. I wasn't sure if it was him casually speaking to a rivaling faction member or the ridiculous trouble he would put others in just to get attention, but I couldn't stand having him around me. Anon taking out Nathaniel was a bold move resulting in us learning about the truth of the game we were in, revealing the wishes that we were apparently fighting for. I knew that Anon had a wish, and if it could send me home... I would be able to murder him for it.

Three Months Before

"You have a 'hit list'?" Zayika's friend, Andrea, asked. "That's not normal."

"Don't tell me what's normal." Zayika pushed down harder on the gas pedal and started taking turns even more sharply.

"I'm going to have to be honest... I don't want to be spending time with you right now and I don't like how you're acting so please let me out of the car." She tried to open her door at the next traffic light, but the vehicle blew right through it.

"Let me out!"

"No. I think you should witness what's about to happen tonight."

"I said let me out!"

Zayika kept driving with increasing speed, knowing exactly where she was heading. "You decided to come along so now you have to deal with what comes next."

The two women approached a house in the suburban neighborhood where they lived. The car came to a screeching halt that gave away their unsettling arrival. After pulling next to a damp curb familiar to Zayika, she went into the glovebox and hastily grabbed a crumpled grey bag. Rainfall was intensifying as the storm they were in grew harsher with each passing minute. She pulled a large knife out of the wrapping and looked over at her friend. There was blood on the blade.

"W-what are you doing?" Andrea reached for the door handle again.

"I'm sending a message."

Zayika abruptly left the driver's side to stomp her way over towards the second story house, knife in hand, and noticed that there were a few lights on. "I'm so happy you're home." she whispered to herself.

Present

It seemed like Omar was trying desperately to understand me. "I'm looking in your eyes right now and it sort of seems like you're almost disappointed that you didn't get to participate in the violence that took place here."

He is right. "I want to prove that I can fight too and earn my ticket home! I followed Nero here because I wanted to get that job done."

"Don't worry about that Zayika. You don't have to prove anything to anyone. Don't get wrapped up in that way of thinking. Let's humble ourselves. Saige and Zekiel are gone now, we are lucky to even still be alive at all. I don't know if there are any other Land Dwellers left now, maybe two or three... if I'm guessing correctly." Omar tried to assure me. "That leaves our faction and the Oceanic Guardians left after them."

It wasn't until he stated that when I realized that my potential fate had been revealed. There were no more wishes remaining–not unless I killed one of my own. *Would that even count?* "Omar, if we can't get wishes from others from our own faction then I have no wish. What if Saige was my only chance?"

He didn't know how to respond at first and kept his mouth closed.

I felt as though the vines of the jungle started to close in and wrap around me as I became lightheaded. "What if I'm stuck here forever? I mean, I like this planet but... I don't want to be held captive!" I felt like I had started spinning.

He pulled me into a comforting embrace and rubbed small circles onto my back. "I'm here for you. We will figure out a way to fix this, just give me some time. I'll try my best. No one else needs to die and no one will be left behind." He told me softly.

"How do you know that this will be okay? Everything is falling apart." *I only care about myself, truly.*

"There has to be some kind of twist here, something that we can figure out to take you home." His eyes suddenly flashed with an idea. "Zayika, what if I wish to take you home with me?"

I felt like my heart was going to beat out of my chest. "Would you really do that for me?" *His innocence is naivety.*

"True friendship means sacrifice."

"I'm shocked that you even see me as a friend. I feel like I haven't gotten to do much here, I haven't been productive with my 'ability' at all. It's a joke."

"Why are you talking about yourself like that?" he asked with a caring heart. "Of course I see you as a friend. When the four of you helped save my life back on the hills and took me in... I will never forget that. You used your ability to heal Anon's leg which was kind of incredible. Plus I hadn't seen anyone use their ability in a pure act of selflessness like that until you fixed him."

"Omar you don't belong here, has anyone told you that?" I gave him a dissatisfied look.

"I get told that all the time." He acted like I sucker punched him in the chest.

"No... that's not what I mean. You're too good for this planet. Your heart, like, you actually care about people.

Your love language is foreign here and it's definitely not welcomed."

"I guess I was brought here for a reason. Maybe the only reason why I'm here is so that I can give you a chance to go back home."

I moved my wavy hair away from my chest and let it flow behind my shoulders. "I want to be honest with you. You don't know me. We met when we arrived here, yes, but Omar I'm not a good person. If you knew the things I've done and thought... you wouldn't even look at me." *Since when am I ever so honest with another person?*

"We have all messed up and will continue to. Human nature is flawed. The best thing we can do to combat that part of ourselves is to be self-aware and improve on the parts of our mind that need to be."

"You're not understanding." I took an intentionally drawn-out pause. "I like the way I am and that's why no one likes me."

"I like you. I like everyone here who is here, messed up or not. I'll bring you home."

"There isn't any other thing that you would want to wish for that would mean more to you than saving me?"

"Zayika I've come from a fairly average life. I'm a commoner, and to an extent I think I will enjoy going back to the simple routines that I have waiting for me at home. I'm going to appreciate my ordinary world more now. What do I want here? I want nothing else than to save a friend. If that's what I'm good for then I won't even hesitate. Plus, as you said when you healed Anon, I do owe you one."

CHAPTER TWELVE: BLUE LIGHTNING, BLUE EVERYTHING

Anon

Present

A vibrant sunset fell over the glistening ocean waves as they rolled to shore. The weather was comforting. For just a moment, I forgot about what was going on around me. It was hard to get the act of killing Nathaniel out of my mind. It would replay in a torturous loop when I attempted to sleep. I tried to not second guess my choices to remind myself that defending others can mean making dire decisions such as that one. I became worried about telling Amira what I did because I didn't want her to see me any differently. There was a piece of me, though, that felt like she was the one and only person who would understand why I did what I chose to do.

I continued walking on firm sand and tried to relish in the unfamiliar tranquility of the planet. Unfortunately, any peace was short lived as I heard a muffled scream off in the distance. I wondered if it was another one of my people that had just died. I decided to keep minding my own business. No matter what I did it was as though trouble always seemed to find me. *How can someone be a leader when there are so many forces working tirelessly against them?* I walked until I arrived at the usual talking spot I had with Amira. I knew that she was expecting me around the time I got there. Within moments she showed up to speak with me again.

"You can't keep meeting with me like this Anon." Amira shook her head as she came out of the water. "You're going to get yourself, or both of us, killed."

"Yes I can. I think you might be my only friend here." I replied as I leaned onto the nearest rock. "Besides we're probably going to die anyways. Why not have a few good conversations before that happens?"

"Since when were you so pessimistic? You know you're a leader, right? Anon, you have to be the brave one here!" She chuckled and tossed a small rock in my direction.

"It's an act that I grow tired of." Our smiles fell in unison at the end of my statement.

"What about Omar and Zayika? You're all in the same faction. Don't you see them as friends?"

"I do... sort of. I enjoy being around them, but I'm not sure they really accept who I am. Zayika doesn't seem to like me but something about her as a person seems troubled in general. I never was off to a steady start with Omar since we banter together more than we collaborate, but I do commend the heart that he does have. He's almost always giving speeches about the morality of humanity and hardly seeing any good left in it. Sometimes that's hard to watch."

"He gives 'speeches'?"

"Amira, he is the only one here that doesn't have any morphed abilities. At first, he was happy about that and now it's as if he is jealous that he doesn't have them too. I don't think he realizes that they are more of a burden than a blessing. Let's say somehow I survive this as the last man standing and get to go home, who is to say that I will get my old body back? Everyone will be horrified by me. I'll most likely get locked up or even killed for being so threatening. Estrella would never talk to me... if she even remembers that I exist."

"Wait, we've had how many talks and I have never heard of a woman named Estrella." Amira splashed water at me and I shook my hands at her.

"Wow, that is what you took from my sad monologue? You heard one woman's name and completely missed my heartfelt speech? To think I was actually going to unlock my complete sad backstory for you to hear at our next meetup." I teased and sat down closer to her.

"Not to pry... but I am kind of curious about where you came from." Her warm brown eyes glistened at me with subtle interest.

"An unhappy marriage and eventual divorce between my parents is the short version. I was talked down to a lot. I'm an only kid. My parents would break my heart over and over again with words and somehow thought that buying me material gifts was supposed to make up for it. Money was love to them and it's also what drove them to not love one another. I'm not going to blame the way they treated me for years for the insecurities that I have, although I can't help but partly feel that way."

"You have a right to acknowledge the damage they did Anon. I'm sorry to hear that is in your past."

I stood up and took off the partial part of a jacket I had to cut and reshape to fit around my wings. While stretching my arms out, I turned and looked at her. "Thanks. As you just said though, it's in the past. I really should move on. I've had strangers treat me better than my own family. I've mainly been taught life lessons by people I hardly know." I took a few seconds before speaking what I felt so compelled to say, "I'm glad I have you here with me on this planet Amira."

One Year Before

The aquarium in the corner of the room bubbled softly as Anon watched many fish swim around in circles. In the silent pauses of his conversation he would count the rocks that were beneath them.

"When do you feel these problems started? The haunting thoughts?" he was asked.

The navy turtleneck sweater he had on felt tight around his neck as he took a deep breath and swallowed, slightly pulling at the fabric. He thought about what to say next. "When I felt like I had failed and that I was at the root of everything falling apart in my life." Anon responded.

"What do you feel you have 'failed' at?" The only other person in the room gave him undivided attention.

"I think I've failed at making strong decisions. I used to have a history of being indecisive and it's... hurt me as my life has gone on so far."

"What about the relationships in your life? Do you feel as though you failed at those?"

"Definitely. I tried to be the best person I could be for everyone at the same time. This isn't saying I was perfect, I hurt many through my actions and words too many times to count." He paused. "Though I think I was so focused on being a good person and looking happy that it wasn't natural. I was forcing a persona that I felt others wanted to see. I honestly wanted to please everyone."

"What did you learn from that?"

"I learned that's completely impossible. No matter what I've done in my life, minor or major, there has always seemed to be at least one person who could disagree with something that I chose. This caused me to overthink so many situations. I've battled this inner fear of not ever feeling like I am enough for what I love in my life and it's all led me to where I am now."

It became silent again between the two sitting across from each other. Anon noticed that one of the fish in the tank had stopped swimming. It was a young blue koi that had stayed eerily still. He felt as though it was staring at him as he watched its eye focus on where he was.

"Let's not only think about the past." The woman looked away from the large window that was behind Anon and shifted her stare directly into his eyes. "Going forward with the knowledge you've gained, what are you going to do to make your future different?"

He looked at the fish as he started to speak, "I'm going to try my best to be a leader. I'll be decisive and quicker on my feet." He then met the gaze of the therapist before he finished saying what he needed to. "I want to be able to make tough calls when they need to be for the right outcome, even if that means letting down someone else, or many others, in the process."

Present

As Amira and I continued our conversation by the ocean shore, the sky grew dark and hazy. Bitterness in the wind swept around and it felt as though a dark presence was approaching us. She began to come out of the water with her legs pushing out of the wet wrap of scales that normally kept them together when she swam. Her morphed state was more restricting than mine since she had to stay near water. I cared for Amira and her safety a lot and was glad that she had a solid companion down in the ocean to help her fight off any other potential threats that would come their way. She didn't act like her morphed changes were a big inconvenience. I didn't either, I knew there was no use in trying to get rid of powers that could help me defend myself. The scales that were just sticking onto her skin were now on the shore being carried out to sea with each wave that came in and went. As I looked at her legs and feet, I saw how scale marks covered her skin and I think she tried to distract me.

"Anon I want to tell you about something I found on a deeper part of the ocean floor." She slicked her wet curls backwards off of her forehead. "Come with me and we can take a walk together."

I followed along beside her, "What did you find?"

"A piece of a large stone. It has engravings on the face of it that tell of magical beings called 'Wish Carriers'."

I lit up. She was the type who got straight to the point. "What did it say?"

"Those who have been called to this planet stemming from a vivid and awakening dream were meant to be here for the reason of guarding a 'wish.' Wishes are meant for those with enough passion and drive for survival to make it back home. In recognition to their bravery at the end of the fight, they are awarded a single wish to grant them anything that they want in life."

I nodded my head as I listened to her words, contemplating how to tell her that I was a Wish Carrier myself. "Wow... that's a lot to take in."

"It is, yes. Anon, I should tell you that I'm a Wish Carrier. I had a dream before I arrived here. I haven't told anyone until you right now." she said.

"You're one too? Why didn't you say anything about your dream back at the bunker with Saige and me?"

"I was really focused on the discovery we were making. I don't know, it sort of slipped by." She ran her fingers nervously against one another, "I'm sorry, I tend to keep to myself and I didn't know any of you well at the time."

"That's okay. I'm glad you told me now, but do you know what this really means for us? It means we're at a much greater risk of getting murdered. I've been on edge even more so ever since I found out. I can't believe they didn't tell us the truth at the opening ceremony."

"Believe me, we will be able to defend ourselves... wait, how did you find out about the Wish Carriers and their meaning? I was deep sea diving in an undiscovered part of the ocean alongside Hippo when I found the broken stone. No one in my faction is aware that I had a dream." She smiled brightly. "I can't believe that you're one too, Anon this is amazing!"

"You remember the man in the bunker?"

"Yes. How could I forget him threatening us?"

"His name was Nathaniel. He came from the Land Dweller faction and was hiding out in that bunker for years. When he was actively fighting for his life just like we are, the stone still stood upright on land. There was an intense storm that broke part of it off and the waves engulfed it."

"When did you talk to him about this? Why didn't you tell me earlier?"

"Omar and I accidentally heard him speaking to Zekiel. I haven't told you yet becau–"

Amira looked at her shaking legs. "I need to get back in the water soon. Sorry, I can't be out of it long. Let's start heading back the way we came."

We continued to walk and all was silent for a few minutes. I was scared to tell her about the murder I committed against Nathaniel, worried that she would react the same way that Omar did.

"So, Amira, I'll just come right out and tell you my truth too since you deserve that." We got closer towards the edge of the ocean as she slowly stepped in. "I killed Nathaniel."

"You did? Why didn't you tell me this at the beginning of our conversation?" Amira fell into the water gently as she got deeper, her body returning to its morphed form.

"I didn't want you to judge me."

"I never knew Nathaniel so don't be worried. I want to hear your side of this. Why did you kill him if he isn't one of the thirty in this fight?" She was remaining surprisingly calm for the news that I just delivered to her.

"How is this not freaking you out?" I asked her cautiously.

"Because I took out three Land Dwellers myself. Well actually Hippo did, but I issued the command that sent her to attack."

"'Three'?" I was shocked.

"Yeah. They were going to kill me."

"Well my kill was technically in self-defense too, in some regard. Nathaniel was prepared to share the stone's information with the rest of the current Land Dweller faction. Saige was already one of their own, which left a giant spotlight on the back of Omar's head and mine as well. I wanted to fight to stay alive and knew that eliminating him would help support the odds of us making it."

"Omar didn't have a dream though. He also wasn't given any morphed abilities. How would he have a wish?"

"Because of the second fact you just stated. He's a complete commoner, an untouched being amongst a sea of morphed misfits. The stone states that those who are entirely human are essentially a walking wish. You didn't read that on the engravings?"

"As I said before, the stone is broken, there's only so much information that I can read from it." Amira paused. "How is Omar doing?"

"I think he is doing okay or at least as well as can be expected. Why do you ask?"

"Don't you see him up there? He's on that rocky ledge at your faction. I'm surprised he even takes walks like that without having the ability to fly."

I looked over and saw what she was talking about. For some reason, Omar was walking dangerously close to the edge and I felt the incessant need to talk him down from there. I flew off in his direction as my heart started to pump faster and faster. I didn't utter one word to Amira as I left, she understood the urgency racing through me.

"Omar! What are you doing? Get back to solid ground!" I reached him and noticed that he was sketching.

"Don't worry, Anon I'll be fine. I'm working on a new piece." he responded casually. "This is what I did back at home. I used to be an artist in case you're wondering."

"Well of course I'm wondering. You had Amira and me worried with you exploring like this, it's dangerous for you okay? I know that we all do it, but this isn't safe for you."

"I'm not a child."

"I know. Look, I'm not trying to talk down to you, but Omar, you can't forget that you don't have powers."

"How could I forget? It seems to be the topic of almost everyone's conversation here. Do you even know what it is like to be the odd one out? To have so many people underestimate you?"

"I do actually."

"See, I'm sorry... but I don't think that you do. I feel like everyone believes I'm a complete sad case. In others' eyes, I'm just an expendable commoner. No one here knows that I do art. You should have seen how surprised you were just now seeing a canvas in my hand." Omar sat down on the ledge with crossed legs.

"Don't take offense to that. No one here really knows the past life of anyone else. Our backstories aren't really that important now." I sat down next to him.

"Of course they are, Anon. Can't you see that everything is connected? You don't think it's our past histories that have brought us here in the first place? We're meant to learn something from this experience."

"Well if your theory is true then I want to know what you have learned." I stared off into the ocean as I spoke, knowing that Amira was watching us from afar.

"I've been humbled. Back in college I wondered why I wasn't part of the popular and successful groups. I didn't feel chosen or important ever. Being here has shown me that it's okay to not be the chosen one. Just because I don't have morphed abilities it doesn't mean that I'm not valuable. In fact, the opposite is true because I don't have any. I'm a walking wish! Only three of us here have wishes. How can I be upset about that?"

His hindsight is admirable.

"I'm glad you've discovered a new perspective."

"I hope that you have too, Anon."

"What is it that you're painting?" I promptly changed the subject. "I'm surprised you even found supplies here for that."

"You'd be surprised by the items that Nathaniel had in his bunker. Although I disagree with what you did to him…" Omar paused and I winced at the memory, "I'm glad I got a chance to see what he had stored away while exploring. He seemed to have been a man of great craftsmanship and creativity with a lot of time on his hands. I'm pretty much making a piece that tells the ending to a painting I made for my class. The unreliable leaky boat that was once out on an unforgiving sea has beaten the odds by reaching the shore at sunset, finally safe from the relentless terrors of the night."

I put my hand on Omar's shoulder. "When we make it out of this, I want you to know that I'm glad we met. We've had our differences, but I do believe we have crossed paths for a reason greater than our own understanding. I do consider you to be my friend and I want you to know that."

"You're my friend too. Although I've disagreed with some of your leadership choices, I will admit that your reasons for them seemed to be rooted from a pure intention to do the right thing in your eyes."

I grinned at him, but he gave me a solemn look in return. "Is something going on?" I asked.

"I wasn't sure how to tell you this... I was putting it off actually... Saige died. Zekiel and Nero are gone too."

I almost lost my balance. "How? When did this happen?"

"I didn't get there in time, well I did, but my words weren't powerful enough against Nero. He hunted them down in the jungle hoping to gain Saige's wish. After he killed her, Zekiel spiraled and tried to attack him but failed. Remember how Gebu told us that there's a fate worse than death for those who lose both wings? He didn't lie."

My mouth went dry. "I don't even know what to say. How did Nero find out about that information?"

"The same way we originally did. Eavesdropping."

It then all clicked in my head as I remembered my conversation with Zayika. "Oh, Nero was there too when we talked."

"Of course he was. He was the person we heard that I followed after and now he's ruined our group. Wait... what do you mean by he was there 'too'?" He saw the answer in my face. "Don't tell me that's why Zayika arrived shortly after me when I got there? She wanted to track down Saige also?"

"Yeah. Once the word got out, this all sort of turned into a free for all, didn't it?"

Omar looked utterly defeated like the last bit of innocence within him had been stolen. "I'm learning more and more every day of what people are capable of doing to others when it comes to prioritizing themselves first."

"Sounds like you gained two perspectives here."

"I don't like the second one."

I nodded in response to him, "You have a strong heart, I will tell you that. Someone couldn't make it as far here as you did without having strength." I decided to fly away to return to Amira.

I wanted to give him space to work on his art and to reflect on the epiphanies of life that he had just shared with me. As I returned to the ocean, I tried to keep my thoughts from straying as my wings helped guide me to the ground. The palms of my hands slowly greeted hot sand as I slightly stumbled with my landing.

"Are you okay?" Amira's sudden attention on me and the stinging on my skin had prevented me from entering a totally zoned-out state.

"Yeah, just thinking about a lot of things right now." I hit my hands together to clean off the dust from the ledge. "Why are you staring at me?"

Amira looked away quickly as I caught her gaze. "What did you talk about with Omar?"

"Our experience here. I think it's catching up to me that the numbers of those alive keep dwindling more and more. We're closer to discovering our fate with each passing minute. Saige and Zekiel are gone."

She didn't look surprised when I told her of the news. "I see. I'm sorry to hear that, they seemed like good people that really cared for one another. Have you made peace with the fate you might receive? Would you be okay with dying here?"

"Why? Are you asking because you're going to… kill me Amira?"

Our eyes locked and widened. We both hardly blinked as we stared at the other. Before we knew it, the two of us were naturally belly laughing at the idea. Humor helped to cope with mourning.

"You're too easy of a kill." she joked at my expense. "Plus, Hippo almost makes killing way too easy in general, I'm sure she could eat lightning itself. I'm ready for a real challenge."

"Be careful what you wish for." I warned her. "I mean if I could have a companion as menacing as yours, I would definitely take it."

"Hippo is sweet. Everyone in my faction seems to be afraid of her, but pretend that they aren't." Amira looked over the ocean as she began to inhale sharply.

"No! Stop! Don't call it over here!" I jumped off of the rock I was resting on. "Why did you name it 'Hippo' anyways?"

"That's my favorite animal. I used to be a wildlife photographer, you know, before I gave up on my dream to pursue someone else's." Amira was clearly amused by what happened based on the tone she was using. "You're not afraid of Hippo too, are you? She's just an anglerfish. I'm sure she wouldn't attack you."

"That's the naivest sentence I've ever heard someone say, which really means something since I'm constantly listening to Omar, and don't get me started on the words that come out of Gebu's mouth."

"Oh come on, just say hi to her. You haven't gotten to officially meet her yet... have you?"

"You've told me a lot of details, so I feel like I have."

Amira called Hippo to come out of the water. Slowly I watched as the anglerfish breached the surface with part of its upper half. It didn't move. The fish had a calming presence, which was somewhat unsettling, but I was thankful that it didn't see me as an enemy. It had black glossy eyes and I saw the familiar stark glow that was emitted by its orb.

"So there's the light that I saw in the ocean." I couldn't help but laugh at some of my previous choices. "Remember when I sought out to discover the phantom lighthouse?"

"Yeah I do." She motioned for Hippo to return to the ocean deep. "She's a great fighting companion and a lot easier to be around compared to my faction members. Those I've been placed with seem to disagree and talk about the most mundane things. What's the rest of your faction like?"

"Well half of them are dead at this point so I wouldn't exactly call them the most valuable players in the game."

Amira's eyebrows furrowed and her pupils grew while looking over at the water again. "Do you feel that?" she asked.

"Feel what?" I gave her a confused expression. "Hey come on, stop joking. I was being serious, don't call your fish all the way over here. Where it was just now was far away enough. I don't want it closing in the extra distance."

"No that's not Hippo, I'm not doing anythi–"

Out of nowhere one of the Oceanic Guardians shot upwards out from the deeper part of the water and started swimming towards Amira.

"If you're smart, you will come underneath the waves with me!" he shouted.

"Orson, what's going on?" Amira's voice was strained.

My throat tightened and the hairs on my skin began standing up. *Something is very wrong.* I looked around to take a mental note of who was nearby. Omar was still up on the cliff, Amira beside me with Orson approaching, and there were two Land Dwellers a bit further away from us who I didn't know. The man from Amira's faction had terror rippling in his eyes.

"Did you not even hear a single word that we talked about during the meeting a few days ago about the forecast? Why don't you listen, Amira? All you do is talk to the enemy who has murdered our own! If you weren't so focused on this irrelevant boy, we could be making progress as a faction!" His voice started making new waves as he swam stiffly.

"Orson calm down." Amira put herself in front of me. "I'm sorry I missed what was said. I wasn't at that meeting. Remember? I went for a late-night swim to gather my thoughts."

Orson got increasingly closer to us before stopping surprisingly in his path. "You have the strongest power out of all of us. You have Hippo. If you paid any attention to anything other than talking to your crush you would realize how dangerous Hippo is to anyone else other than you. We all could be home by now if you would just focus and get the killing done!"

"Now is not the time to fight." she responded. "Why did you tell me to go underwater?"

"How can you miss so much of the information that our stone has to share with us?" Orson screamed in frustration. "It's not like you're a Wish Carrier or someone who can break the rules. You know what the representative said at the opening ceremony–groups need to fight together if we want to make it through this."

"Wish Carriers are here, though, you know that right?" I chimed in. Amira looked displeased with me. *She doesn't want them knowing.*

"There are none, you foolish outsider. Half of the stone's lore is outdated, only the other half is relevant, and it's currently headed our way! Not like you would even know what I'm talking about!" Orson yelled at me.

From the depths further out, another merman arose. "Get down here now! Both of you! You can kill the other factions after the earthquake! Come on!"

"I'm coming, Marcellus!" Orson responded as he gave Amira one last loaded look. "I can't believe I've risked my life to save the most unhelpful and distracted member of our faction."

As he disappeared under the water, Amira and I turned to one another.

"This couldn't be the same type of incident like when the stone was first destroyed?" Her worried expression fell into almost despair as she looked behind me. "Oh no, it has to be an... earthquake."

"What are you looking at?" I spun around and was reminded that Omar was on a cliff's ledge.

The noise of the ocean thrashing began to encompass us. My feet were unsteady as I tried to hold my balance on sand.

"There's no time." Amira's eyes started to cascade with tears. She turned around to dive into the next oncoming wave.

Out of my peripheral vision I could see the two Land Dwellers starting to yell and heading in the direction of Nathaniel's old bunker to take cover. I could feel my own blood pulsing and rushing through my body as I flew upwards with great force away from the planet's surface beneath me. Within seconds a loud noise rang through the tense air. I began to watch our faction's platform crumbling as Omar was shouting incoherent words on it. Before I could even blink, he started to fall. The foundation beneath his feet had cracked and left no reaction time for either of us to diffuse the series of events that happened next. I felt as though I was choking on my own tongue as I flew desperately in the direction of his plummeting body.

"Omar!" I called out as I watched him hit the ground at the speed of light.

"What's happening?" I heard Gebu call out as he peered over the rumbling edge and called over another one of our faction's members to join him. "Mae, something has happened! We have to help Omar! Make sure you're charged up. We might need healing down here."

I rushed to his side and landed in his spewing blood. I examined his body and found that the back of his skull had split open upon impact. I placed the back of my hand against my mouth as I began to sob. I bent down and grabbed his ruptured head and my entire being went numb. A force of nature came over me. Everything turned blue. The sky was blue, the cliffs were blue, my hand and Omar's blood was blue. *What is happening?* I looked up to see if Gebu and Mae were still at the top of the rocks. They weren't there. I called out Amira's name and heard nothing in return. It was as though Omar's body and I were the only two on the planet. I yelled out for help and only received more silence.

Wind started to pick up around me, it sounded like many whispers of haunted souls asking for forgiveness and healing. A ray of lightning bolted through the sky past mountains and down into the ocean. A loud roar rattled from the harrowing waters. *Is that Hippo?* I couldn't see her light in the waters. "This isn't okay. What you did is not okay. This will follow you for forever Anon." Omar was talking, repeating the words he spoke to me when he found out I killed Nathaniel. I looked down and saw his eyes roll backwards as he started crying blood. I jolted backwards and dropped his head to the ground when I heard what he said. *This can't be happening.* I stood up and spun around in a circle, looking at the planet changing before my eyes. Everything was wrong and had flipped on its own head. Darkness spread across the land and sky as the whispers continued. *I have to get out of here...* I tried to stand up and start flying away but an invisible power was holding me down.

"Hello Anon." Zayika was up on the cliff and she looked different. The blue sky began pouring over with stars of all shapes and sizes. "I learned that I can not only heal with stars, but, I can do a lot of damage with them too." The manner in which she was carrying herself was vile.

"What is going on?" I tried to ask her. As I looked into her eyes, it was as if a mask had slipped off her skin. The woman who was before me was a complete stranger, one that oozed corruptness. She wore a dress of stars, threatening both my sanity and existence.

"You will learn what I am capable of because of what you've done to me. Actions should have consequences. Negligence needs to be reprimanded, especially against those who are being mindfully inconsiderate."

"What? I don't know what you're talking about!" Another ray of lightning plummeted downwards. Everything went bright.

"Are you okay?" Someone spoke to me and pulled me out of whatever trance I was in. I pushed my fingers against my eyes roughly to rub them as I looked around again. Everything went back to how it was. Omar's eyes were still and lifeless like they were, no tears of blood, only the bleeding from the fall that he originally had. The colors of the sky had faded back to normal and I started to tremble. I was still sitting with him on my lap.

"What's going on?" Mae yelled over the piece of the cliff that was still remaining. "Gebu and I will try to find a way down!"

"Did you forget I can fly?" Gebu responded offendedly.

"I actually did. Your wings are so small sometimes I forget they are there."

"Can both of you stop talking?" I shouted at them with pure rage in my voice. "He is dead! Show some decent respect!" I didn't sound like myself.

Gebu leaned further over the edge than he had been and finally saw the full picture. I was holding Omar's broken body in my lap and his blood seemed to have covered every inch of me. I leaned my head down towards his as my tears fell onto his lifeless face. The planet's earthquake around us had stopped, but it felt as though it transferred inside of me. I heard a body frantically come out of the water but I refused to turn around.

"Anon, what happened?" I heard Amira's voice.

"I'm over here." I tried to speak but I felt too weak to raise my voice loud enough for her to hear me.

Even though I was surrounded by large rocks and several jagged parts of the cliff, Amira found her way to me as fast as she could.

"No…" she managed to say as she saw the gruesome scene in front of her.

I couldn't stop crying as I held onto what used to be Omar. My mind involuntarily replayed all of the moments in my mind when I wasn't the friend I should have been to him. I instantly felt disdain for the ability I was given. All I wanted was the opportunity to turn back time and fix the nightmare that was before me. Three from our original group had their lives ripped away selfishly and unfairly. I eventually looked up at Amira as she put her hands gently on my shaking shoulders to comfort me.

"You can't run away now." I heard someone whisper. "Their guard is finally down, let's just get this over with."

"Who's there?" Amira asked as she stood up confidently. "There's no use in hiding! You will be found!"

"Amira look out!" Gebu had a bird's eye view and warned us from above. "There's two Land Dwellers nearby!"

I nodded my head as I spoke directly to her. "They are the last two of that faction left. Once they're dead, we are even closer to winning this." I took Omar's head off of my legs and placed him gently on the small bed of rocks I was on.

"They're the last two? Really?" she asked.

"Yeah. I haven't seen any others besides the both of them." A few more tears raced one another down my face as I kept my eyes off of Omar.

"I know you were his friend and I'm sure this is devastating right now, but Anon, you need to think clearly in order to survive right now."

"I know. I'm tired." *I am so tired...* "We need to finish this."

Amira put her hand on my cheek and we put our foreheads softly against one another. "Let's finish this then."

"We both have to go back to Earth, not just one of us." I informed her.

"How do you plan on doing that? We aren't from the same faction." she asked quietly, her skin still on mine. "It's messed up but we can't spare one another and still use our wish too. If there's one thing that the representatives were truthful about, it's that those who return do have to be from the same faction."

"Are you serious? Are you sure?" I asked her.

"I've had a lot of time underwater. I gained a lot of knowledge there."

We kept our voices low with the bridges of our noses brushing together. "I will spare your life with my wish then. If we can't break the rules, then we can navigate around them."

"What if I spare you first with mine?" she responded.

"I'm not letting you. I know you have a wish deep down inside of your soul that you should ask for instead."

"How do you know that?"

"I have read between the lines of our conversations." I pushed a few of her tight curls away from her face. "Let's go."

The two of us took deep breaths as we carefully stepped over a mess of rocks. Amira gave me a look that silently told me that we should pursue different directions for approaching our enemies. I gave her a quiet expressive response in return as I knelt down and crawled closer to where we first heard their voices.

"Fabian, we don't stand a chance. Almost our entire faction is dead." I heard one of them say.

"The two of us still have a chance to win this, though." The other responded. "Hurry up and craft your weapon. I would if my ability wasn't just creating useless smoke grenades. You need to alter your defeated mindset."

"Come on dude, your ability is super useful. We can stun and flank them with those right now if you weren't so busy judging me."

"Okay we can't turn against one another. That's exactly what they want." Fabian huffed.

As they came into my view, I noticed that their backs were facing me. Both men were too distracted by the other's words to keep their own guard up. Without a second thought I lunged forwards to the one on my right and got him in a headlock.

"Who? Where did you come from?" I was asked. I could only hear fear in his voice.

"I'm Anon. I was behind those rocks over there from the earthquake."

"Please let go of Fabian." he tried to plead with me, "You don't get it! He's my only friend here. I don't think I can win this without him."

"You shouldn't rely solely on others. You have to fight for yourself." I told him as I tightened my grip. I noticed Amira sneaking up behind Draydon as I tried to keep distracting him with my words. "You know what power I have, right? I'm sure you saw me in your courtyard when I killed Nathaniel. In just an instant I can electrocute Fabian here so keep that in mind if you plan on attacking me."

Amira ran up behind Draydon and placed her hand over his mouth. He saw the faded scales all over her hands and began panicking as they brushed against his parted lips. Fabian stayed silent as he watched the events unfolding, my arm almost cutting off his airway.

"So what happens ne–" I began to ask Amira, but before I could finish my sentence she had already snapped the neck of Draydon. She wasted no time and carefully strategized every move that she made.

"What are you taking your time with Anon? Finish him." Her words sounded guilty and broken, but also direct and calculated.

With her instruction I sent a surge of lightning through both of my arms and she moved back from me while watching. My skin stung again, like the first layer of it was peeled off, a feeling I'd unfortunately become somewhat used to after using my powers as many times as I did. With closed eyes, I killed Fabian. His lifeless body placed a weight on me that I almost couldn't withstand. I wanted nothing more than to finally save my progress in the game I was in, return to Earth, and never touch it again.

"Who's left?" I asked Amira as I let his body go.

"I think there are two of mine and three of yours." She made the screwed-up situation sound like poetry. "Let's round them all here and get this over with."

"How are we going to play our cards? We're supposed to be enemies. Everyone knows that we aren't and they probably hate us because we don't hate each other. I mean look at Orson, he was so upset that you spend time with me. You've probably spent more time talking to me than anyone else in your faction. Why is that?"

"Yes, that's because I have no desire to get to know them Anon. I think I was called here to find my inner peace. Up until now I've always been a lone wanderer, traveling and taking photos of each of my single steps. I was in need of finding a friend and I've been led straight to you. It's our duty to see to it that we both make it out of this. We both are more than capable of pulling through the worst. That doesn't mean we take joy in the killing we have done, don't let this game cause you to question who you are. We have to do what it takes to protect ourselves and those we are connected to. This planet seems to be all about overcoming our personal issues so that we can see the full picture and clearer understanding of our own self-perception. We play our cards by expanding our creativity and critical thinking."

"You learned a lot about this planet from the stone, didn't you?" I asked her. "You're definitely an investigator, I will give you that. What else did you learn?"

"I learned that the name of this planet is Eunoia. After each Wish Carrier completes their personal duty Eunoia, after all of its callings, is designed to advertently create a society back on Earth that has a well mind and exhibits beautiful thinking with those who survived and returned."

"You memorized that?"

"Hippo likes to be read to." She took both of my hands in hers. "The word eunoia consists of six letters and only five of them are vowels... one letter isn't. There were six of us at the beginning."

"What does that mean?" I thought briefly. "Wait... Omar? He was the only one of us six with no ability."

Amira's eyes looked solemn. "This was all meant to happen. This is the end, well, hopefully it is."

"What happened?" Zayika's voice tore through and completely broke the melancholy atmosphere. "Where is Omar?" Her words sounded like screams that rang in my ears.

Amira and I watched as she scrambled down to the ground away from our faction. Gebu and Mae followed closely behind her.

"There was an earthquake, you didn't feel it?" Gebu made things worse.

"No one told me what was going on! I was in my room. Why didn't anyone call me?" Zayika sprinted towards the location where Omar died.

"We were going to tell you, Zayika. Things were just really intense out here." I tried to explain. When I looked at her, I felt ill. For some reason... I wanted to get as far away from her as I possibly could. "Why did you have that conversation with me? Why was the planet in ruins and... blue?"

"I don't know what you are talking about, Anon." she bellowed in my direction as Omar's body laid in front of her scuffed shoes. I decided to not bring up the trance again. "Why did he have to die? I was supposed to get his wish! Damn it!"

Does she only care about her own self?

"We just fought off the remaining Land Dwellers." Amira chimed in.

"Who asked you? By the way, shouldn't you be dead Amira? Have you all lost your minds?" Zayika looked at everyone on the beach's shore in awe. "All of us standing here are from the Over Grounds faction besides Amira. Why isn't she dead yet?"

"She's been with us from the start." I walked over by her side.

"Who cares? Maybe if you weren't so busy defending a mermaid with a horrific mutated fish then Omar might still be alive."

"Omar's death was no one's fault." As I spoke, I could feel the dried traces of tears down my face. "We didn't know the earthquake was coming. There was no time to react."

"Well, Anon, you sure do seem to find enough time to react when it only conveniences you. Nathaniel seemed to get murdered pretty quickly."

I felt a painful lump grow in my throat when I heard her comment. "You don't have to make this personal, Zayika."

"Every poor decision you've now made as our 'leader' has been personal." Her eyes shifted their focus towards Amira. "So, do you want to end your own life yourself or let one of us do it for you? Someone who has more tenacity than Anon."

Gebu and Mae shifted their weight in the sand uncomfortably during the conversation.

"I don't think many of us here have as much tenacity as him. I even ran from the last fight, which I'm sorry about that guys." Gebu kicked his foot around nervously.

"We all mess up sometimes." I assured him. "Thanks for the compliment by the way."

"Here come the last two." Mae stated as she pointed towards Orson and Marcellus coming out of the water. They both had merman tails that had started changing once the air hit them.

"Amira stop talking to them! We have to fight them!" Orson started a determined run after his tail finally shifted back to human leg form. He tripped, but eventually picked up a steady pace.

Orson was carrying a heavy metal weapon resembling a hammer and targeted Gebu first. The tool he was holding slipped from his hands, which were wrinkly and soft due to such great amounts of water exposure. The hammer ended up flying from his hands and hit Gebu in his throat and upper chest area. We all heard him start heaving as he grabbed himself in distress.

"You shouldn't have done that!" Mae yelled at him as she bolted towards Orson and wrapped a glowing string around his neck several times. "Suffer the fate you have casted."

Orson's face was turning purple as he suffocated. Long range shots were being sent off from a bow and arrow crafted by Marcellus. Amira quickly checked on Gebu as Mae and I started dodging the rusty arrows aimed at us.

"He's gone." Amira stood up and ran back closer to us.

"So is he." Mae announced Orson's death.

I flew up into the air to even the fighting field on Marcellus, who was closer to the water than the rest of us. I charged up a new surge within myself to target him. His reflexes were faster than most of those I had fought as he narrowly missed each ray of lightning I directed to strike him. He sent an arrow to hit Mae after seeing Orson dead. He got her and I was able to hit him in return. Rays of blue and white bounced across the ocean's surface as I took his life.

"We did it!" I heard Zayika announce. "Except Amira is still here. Anon, are you going to finish this or am I going to?"

I took her threat seriously and flew back down in between the two women. "I would kill you before I would allow you to hurt Amira."

"I can defend myself." Amira tried to say.

"I'm not willing to risk it, okay?" I tried to be calm and look back at her.

"We're being watched." Zayika refocused our attention.

Up on the hill there were three silhouettes facing us. The representatives. The tone of a peaceful trumpet rang out over all of us as we watched them from afar. Seeing them was calming, almost as if they were bringing a ray of hopefulness along with them to offer us who were down below.

"The three of you have made it to the finish line." It was the representative of the Over Grounds faction speaking. "But only two of you can cross."

"What do you mean by that?" Zayika asked.

"Only two wishes remain, and they are held by Anon and Amira who were given them by default. Congratulations to you two for holding onto them."

"Amira has a wish?" Zayika looked angry. "I was supposed to have one. Omar promised his for me!"

"That doesn't matter because he is dead now." The representative told her. "We can see that there is some controversy surrounding your friendship with Amira, Anon. It seems that you're willing to defend her life even though she is the enemy?" She walked into a ray of sunlight, a small smile could be seen planted on her face. "You're aware that you both can't go back to Earth with your wishes, rivaling factions can't return side by side, unless you use your choice to save her."

I tried to speak but I couldn't.

"You're not going to pick Amira over me, right Anon?" Zayika grew more upset. "It's not like you'd waste your wish on her."

"What is it you are choosing, Amira?" she was asked. "You might want to make your decision quickly, we don't want you to return to your morphed state while you're not near the water."

Amira grabbed my hand and held onto it steadily as she spoke. "I want the waterfall destroyed."

Disbelief beamed from my representative's face, "How do you know about the waterfall? Yo-you're not supposed to know about that." She looked regretful for stating her initial response. "I mean, what are you talking about? Where is this waterfall located?"

Amira looked sure of herself. "You know what I'm talking about. You know it's tied to this planet, Eunoia, along with the string of incidents and lost lives that take place around it. I want it gone without a trace of its existence left over, that is my wish."

"How do you know the planet's name?"

"I'm not sure I'm required to tell you that." Amira stood and squared her shoulders proudly.

"You should wish for something else, truly. You could wish for anything under the sun. Please reconsider this decision."

The representative from the Land Dweller faction was shaking his head frantically. "Amira - please change your wish."

"No."

"Please–" he begged.

"No."

All of the heads of each faction took a moment to huddle together and speak out of earshot from Amira, Zayika, and me.

"Anon how did you not tell me that she had a wish?" Zayika glared.

"It was none of your business." Amira responded for me.

"Don't you dare try to tell me what my business is you self-righteous–"

"Enough." I cut her off.

"Upon careful thought and reflection, we have come to the consensus that Amira's wish... will be granted." The Oceanic Guardians faction leader walked over to the three of us. "We will keep our promise of granting any wish, whatever it may be, even though we strongly... we strongly... advise you against choosing this, Amira."

"I stand by what I asked for." She gave me an encouraging nod.

The attention was now on me. "It's time for a decision, Anon. What will your wish be?"

I looked at Zayika and Amira. I cared for both of them, I really did. I truly wanted nothing but success for the two of them in their lives going forwards. With the situation I was put in, I had no choice but to pick one or the other to return with me. Yes, Amira had her own wish, but we were from rivaling factions. There was no way for her wish to be granted until one of us killed the other. I could barely stomach the thought of this let alone truly ending her life. "My wish..." *What if I have failed as a leader? As a friend?* I bit my lip. *What did Omar's words mean? What did that blue trance mean?* I closed my eyes. *Have I failed my own self?*

"Go on." The representative replied anxiously. "Please, Anon, time is being wasted."

"I wish for Amira's life to be spared on this planet, resulting in her being allowed to return home despite being from another faction."

Zayika immediately fell downwards with her knees hitting the rocky terrain. "Anon..."

I looked directly into her eyes despite not wanting to, "What?" I asked desperately.

"You... You're leaving me behind?" I watched as her hopes crumbled.

"I can't take both of you." I stated.

"We're from the same faction. How could you do this to me? Do you know how many times I've saved your pathetic life?" Her voice became louder.

Amira tucked her arm underneath mine. "He made his choice, Zayika. Not everyone gets what they want."

Zayika's mouth fell open. "You can't leave me here! I'm going to lose my mind, my identity, and my future. What am I supposed to do?"

The Over Grounds representative spoke up. "You will wait for the other humans who will be brought here. You will wait until each faction becomes whole again with ten members."

"When will that be?" she responded instantly.

"Their calling can't be predicted. When it's destined to be, they will arrive."

"Will they be Wish Carriers?"

"We don't know. It's rare that as many of them appeared in your group during this time."

"So you're telling me that I can be stuck here for years? Even if after waiting for others to arrive, I may be killed regardless? Or miss out on getting a wish again?"

"Yes, you're correct." The representative turned towards me as Zayika began wailing out in despair behind her. "Congratulations Amira and Anon. You're going to make it home."

Zayika propped herself up with her dirty and bruised hand. "Amira, wait, please give me a chance. Give me a ticket home, I'm begging you. Use your wish on me like Anon did for you. I promise that I will find a way to repay you."

"No." Amira responded. "I already made my choice."

Zayika's eyes then seemed to change from sadness to a sinister nature. "Well if I kill you right now then I will get your wish."

I stepped in between them once more and as my arms lit up abruptly. I held rays of sharp lightning at the edge of my fingertips and pointed them at Zayika. "I won't let you."

"You will regret this Anon. I will never forget you." Zayika spoke hauntingly. "I promise that I will find a way to make you regret this."

Zayika's words made it feel as though she casted a spell on me.

I turned to face Amira and with a hopeful but heavy chest I spoke, "It's time for us to go back."

"Yes, it's time." Amira looked at the ocean with a cordial expression as if she was saying goodbye to her anglerfish.

The representative put her arm up high into the air and a burst of light swept over the Eunoia as we both were taken back to Earth.

THE END

NOVEL EXTRA: CHARACTER POEMS

AMIRA
Quiet Confidence
A steady walk in,
names are thrown slandering them.
The tongue stays held back.

ZEKIEL
Familiarity
A moment in blue,
cold and eerie déjà vu.
I've been here before,
teleportation devastation.
To go back and fix this moment,
would evict this lonely hue.

ANON
On the Edge
With my back turned away from my home I stared into
the distance. Off the rocky shore lay a vast and angry
ocean ahead of me. Conflict was in the air as smoky
clouds loomed over my presence. My hair blew over my
eyes and my clothes grew colder around me. Each
moment of passing time attacked me as I tried to kill it
and intrusive thoughts trespassed and violated my hopes
for the future.

SAIGE
Unspoken Words
I need to see you run.
I need to see you breathe.
Because I hold my breath,

when you drift away from me.

ZAYIKA
Fabric
It feels like a tangled piece of fabric is expanding in my
head,
I don't know how to untangle it.
The only way to do so is to gouge my eyes out and lose
sight of myself in the process.

OMAR
Cloud Break
It's terrifying how fast the clouds are falling,
running through the mist with blind eyes.
Arms swinging frantically,
fingertips only met with cold air that pierces them.
Trembling lips with an aching head that directs them to
stop moving,
the only direction taken is backwards with an ill
tongue.